ALTERNATE SIDES

BOOKS BY MARISSA PIESMAN

ALTERNATE SIDES

CLOSE QUARTERS

HEADING UPTOWN

PERSONAL EFFECTS

UNORTHODOX PRACTICES

THE YUPPIE HANDBOOK (WITH MARILEE HARTLEY)

ALTERNATE
SIDES

A NINA FISCHMAN MYSTERY

MARISSA PIESMAN

Delacorte Press

ΛγS

Published by
Delacorte Press
Bantam Doubleday Dell Publishing Group, Inc.
1540 Broadway
New York, New York 10036

Library of Congress Cataloging in Publication Data

Piesman, Marissa.
Alternate sides / Marissa Piesman.
p.   cm.
ISBN 0-385-31355-1
I. Title.
PS3566.I4235A58   1995
813'.54—dc20   94-24156
CIP

Manufactured in the United States of America
Published simultaneously in Canada

August 1995

10 9 8 7 6 5 4 3 2 1
BVG

I would like to thank Carole Berry for brainstorming with me while I was in a postnatal haze. It seems that I can always use some help with plots in my life. I'm also grateful to my editor, Jackie Farber, my publicist, Candice Chaplin, and all the rest of the great folks at Delacorte Press. My agent, Janet Wilkens Manus, and my husband, Jeffrey Marks, have continued to lend guidance, inspiration, and support. And special thanks go to my daughter for being such a good kid.

ALTERNATE SIDES

CHAPTER 1

It was Thursday night and Nina was on the crosstown bus going in the wrong direction. Not that she didn't mean to end up on Third Avenue, but going to the East Side always made her feel as if she was headed the wrong way. She didn't really mind going over to Jonathan's apartment all the time. He had all those things that you were supposed to have—cable television, a dishwasher, an air conditioner, a kitchen counter. And it was pleasant to spend Saturday morning with a cappuccino machine and the *New York Times* delivered to your door, the magazine and book review sections already neatly tucked inside.

It had been years since she had gotten the *Times* delivered, back when she had roommates and lived in a building that the *Times* would bother with. In those days, the Saturday paper was the runt of the litter, the skinniest edition of the week. Now it came packed with half of the next day's offering, presumably so that all the overachievers in town would have more time to study it before they showed up for work on Monday morning.

You really could spend the whole weekend reading the Sunday paper, if you were willing to bother with things like reviews of science fiction novels and the Q&A in the real estate section. Nina never read the Q&A, since the Q's were always from angry New York City tenants, any of whom could be one of Nina's clients. She got enough kvetching from them during the week, she didn't need it with her cappuccino.

It was tempting to spend the day with the *Times*, now that she had a boyfriend. Being in a relationship was proving to be relaxing, mainly because it cut down on all that time she used to spend trying to meet men. Well, not actually trying to meet men, but trying to get herself to try to meet men. And the endless hours of . . . well, not self-improvement in the traditional sense, like taking courses or getting your eyebrows waxed. But every time she went out with someone new, she'd have to spend the following week dissecting their interaction with each of her friends. And then, of course, she'd have to reciprocate whenever one of them met someone. It was easier to stay home and read the paper.

But Jonathan's apartment wasn't home. That was starting to be a problem. He had asked her to move in and had been upset when she put him off. Not that she didn't want to live with him. For one thing, she wouldn't mind being in a cohabitational state by age forty, with which she was facing a head-on collision. For another thing, she loved him. At least she supposed she did. With someone like Nina Fischman it was hard to tell. Ambivalence had been the keynote speaker at all of Nina's internal monologues for as long as she could remember. So while she waited for shivers down her spine and accelerated heartbeats, all she felt was a warm melt that might be love but also might only be gratitude at having a living mammal to press up against at night.

But it wasn't this confusion that was preventing her from making the move. It had nothing to do with him, she had explained. Or the fact that it was his home turf. And she actually liked the way he had fixed the place up. Some women might find it too bachelorish, with its Hunt Club browns and greens, nothing frothy or floral. But Nina wasn't the frothy type. She wasn't the decorating type at all. In fact, Jonathan's apartment looked far better than any space Nina had ever been responsible for. She really had no good reason for not wanting to move in except that she just couldn't picture herself living in that building.

For one thing, it was on the wrong side of the park. She'd admit that she could imagine living on the East Side under certain circumstances. Nina could easily have been seduced eastward by a charming brownstone perched atop Carnegie Hill or a garden duplex facing the Frick. Or even a one-bedroom in a sensible mid-block prewar, thirteen stories or so, where middle-class New Yorkers lived out their rent-sta-bilized lives and sent their children to P.S. 6. But Jonathan lived in a low IQ building.

He lived in a rental in the eighties, on the corner of Third Avenue, what was referred to as a luxury high-rise. It rose pretty high and Nina supposed that a doorman and two ele-vators that broke down infrequently constituted luxury. But it wasn't as if they were handing out steaming towels at the door. And she could have lived without the smoked-glass mirrors that lined the lobby.

She didn't think she was being unreasonable. She wanted them to make a life together, or at least what was left of one. Could you make a life together once you were past forty? Wasn't what you were making really only half a life?

Besides, Jonathan knew it was a low IQ building. He'd go on for hours about the toupees and exposed chest hair he'd see in the elevator. "For Chrissakes," he'd say. "Didn't any-one around here ever wonder why their shirts have buttons that go all the way up to the neck? What do they think they're there for, decoration?"

Jonathan did not fit in among the chest hair brigade. Not only did he button his shirts all the way to the neck, but he rarely even rolled up his shirtsleeves. Which was what had made Nina notice him last summer out in Fire Island, among all that exposed flesh. He clearly did not belong in this glitzy postwar tower and he knew it. Nina suspected that the real reason that Jonathan did not want to give up his apartment was Ray the doorman. Ray worked the day shift and for a certain sum he would move your car across the street to comply with alternate side of the street parking regulations. He performed this duty for a small and select group of tenants, and it had taken Jonathan years to move up and off Ray's waiting list. Whatever he paid the doorman, it was well worth it, since the local monthly garage rates were three hundred bucks plus.

Nina hadn't even suggested that Jonathan consider moving into her apartment. For starters, it had none of the things an apartment was supposed to have, not even a kitchen counter. Not even a kitchen, really. A sink, refrigerator and stove lined one wall of the living room. She supposed that some women dreamed of gleaming expanses of Formica, some dreamed of Corian, some dreamed of marble and granite. Nina dreamed of having someplace to chop an onion.

Her building was the antithesis of luxury, while simultaneously managing not to convey any character. Tucked away in the West Seventies, which featured such architectural treasures as the Ansonia and the Apthorp, it was a dull four-story tenement. The kind of building that you could find anyplace on the East Coast where there was once a need to house the urban working poor. In Manhattan these days you had to have a graduate degree to earn enough money to afford housing that had been built for the urban working poor. Nina knew that despite the fact that she was a lawyer and had a job she was nothing more than a nineties' version of New York's working poor. After her rent and psychotherapy bills, there was hardly anything left over. A new fall wardrobe typically consisted of panty hose, a haircut and a fresh tube of hand cream for the approaching winter.

She had always thought that when she finally did move in with someone, they would make their home on West End Avenue or Riverside Drive. But that fantasy had been formed back when those streets were considered a bohemian alternative to Park Avenue. Before the neighborhood became populated by people who attended Dartmouth and worked for banks. You didn't buy an apartment on West End or Riverside casually anymore. Just getting past the co-op board could take months. Things were easier back in those *Barefoot in the Park* days when young couples would rent something small and fun and move in the next day with their folding chairs. Today if you found something available immediately, it might be small, but it was not going to be fun.

Since Jonathan was content to stay put, it seemed to be up to Nina to find someplace for them to move. This coming weekend, she told herself, she would call some brokers and scour the ads. Meanwhile, she had this evening at Jonathan's to look forward to. Thursday night was television night and Chinese food night. Her mood brightened as her mind turned from real estate to the NBC lineup and Dumpling House's take-out menu.

Maybe she should just give up her West Side fixation already, she thought as she walked up Third Avenue from the Seventy-ninth Street bus stop. After all, the Chinese restaurants on Second Avenue were as good as the ones on Broadway. Besides, it would be nice to have a doorman, especially one who moved your car. And by now all of her favorite stores had East Side branches—Arche, Eileen Fisher, even

Putumayo. You could dress like a genuine West Sider without ever going west of Madison.

Though Jonathan's building lacked character, it did give Nina a feeling of control. Everything always looked the same. The lobby was never too hot or too cold and the marble floor was always polished. Jonathan's apartment always had that day's *Times* folded neatly on the coffee table and there was always milk in the refrigerator. You knew what to expect. Except that today, upon entering Jonathan's apartment, instead of finding darling little cardboard containers of vegetable dumplings and moo shu pork, she found two strange men sitting on the couch. And they did not look as if they were delivering Chinese food. They looked like plainclothes police officers. Which they were.

"What's going on here?" she whispered to Jonathan, after he followed her into the bedroom.

"You're never going to believe this. One of the doormen was murdered."

"So what are these guys doing in your apartment? Were you there when it happened?"

"No, but it was Ray. And he happened to be parking my car at the time he was killed."

"Oh my God. So they found him in your car?"

"That's right."

"You don't think you're a suspect, do you?"

"I don't know what to think. They haven't read me my Miranda rights or anything."

Miranda. Such a pretty name for such a sordid business. Nina pulled her mind back to the problem at hand. "Well, what kind of questions are they asking you?"

"Where I was this morning, that kind of thing."

"That doesn't sound good."

"Here we go again."

"I know." They had spent the last summer extricating

Jonathan from implication in the murder of his oldest friend. For a nice cuddly Jewish guy who had gone to art school and worked for an advertising agency, he certainly knew a lot of homicide victims.

"I better go back out," he said. "But start thinking of who we should call just in case . . . you know."

Nina's mind raced. She tried frantically to remember the names of all of the criminal lawyers who were friends of friends, of bail bondsmen, of what she should do next. But first things first. "In that case," she said, "we'd better set the VCR."

CHAPTER 2

By the time they got around to thinking about whether to watch the tape of that night's "Seinfeld" episode, it was after midnight. "Forget it," Jonathan said. "We'll watch it over the weekend."

"No," Nina insisted. "I want to watch it now."

"But I'm really tired."

"I can imagine. Being grilled by the cops all those hours. You poor thing." She walked around to the back of the couch and gave him a brief head massage, then moved down to his shoulders. She knew that he expected her to continue moving downward, but some irresistible impulse led her away from his back over to the VCR. She pushed the rewind button. "You can go to bed, if you want," she said. I'll be there in half an hour. Minus commercials."

"Nina . . ."

"Look, if I don't watch 'Seinfeld' immediately . . . well, I know myself. I'll either have to get up early to watch it or be late for work. And getting up early is too painful and getting to work late is too disruptive. So I might as well watch it now." She plopped herself down on the couch next to Jonathan and waited for the tape to finish rewinding.

"Why can't you wait for the weekend?"

"Because I can't. All day tomorrow, people will be coming up to me in the office asking me if I saw last night's episode. And if I say no, they'll go ahead and tell me about it in great detail so by the time I get to see it, it'll seem like a rerun. Not only that, but I'll be obsessing about whether or not we'll be able to schedule the time to watch and if we don't get to see it until Sunday night, I'll have wasted the entire weekend worrying."

"We'll watch it, we'll watch it. For Godssakes, you're a real nut case." He seemed to say it with genuine irritation, not affection, but Nina flushed with pleasure nonetheless. Because it was such a luxury to get to be the difficult one in the relationship for a change. At least every now and then. Not to have to be terrified that one wrong word would send him racing out the door, never to come back. There had been so many of them who *had* raced out and hadn't come back. Her entire life as an adult sexual being could be summed up in a single freeze frame of some guy looking over his shoulder, waving good-bye.

And now there was Jonathan, who could be summed up in a single freeze frame of a guy sitting on a couch with his shoes off eating Chinese food. The guy she had been waiting for all her life. Except instead of being totally blissed out, she noticed these prima donna instincts erupting within her. Like having to watch "Seinfeld" *now* even though it was practically one o'clock in the morning. And not wanting to move into Jonathan's apartment, even though she had to admit there was nothing really wrong with it.

Although now that Ray had been murdered, Jonathan didn't have anyone to park his car for him. Which meant that he might be more open to the thought of moving. Some good might come out of this killing after all. She felt guilty for having the thought, but she couldn't pretend that she was exactly grief-struck. She'd known Ray only slightly, and he had made Nina nervous, the way he sniffed around Jonathan like a dog, trying to smell out opportunities for making extra money. Parking his car, getting his mail, feeding his cat. And Jonathan wasn't exactly a cash cow, having spent much of the previous year collecting unemployment insurance. But he was back at his former ad agency, doing a series of illustrations for a campaign about some breakfast cereal. Agency billings were up and it looked as if he'd be around for a while. Although things were never that secure in the volatile advertising industry. The loss of a big client often meant layoffs.

"Are you going to have to move the car tomorrow morning?" she asked. Moving the car meant hitting the street by seven, since it usually took an hour to find a legal space.

"No, the police took care of that for me. They've taken it away."

"What are they going to do with it?"

"I don't know. Search it for clues, I guess. Fingerprints, hair samples, all that kind of stuff."

"Was the guy who shot Ray sitting in the car with him? Assuming it was a guy."

"Nina, you sat here the whole time they were questioning me. Weren't you listening to anything they said?"

"Yeah, I was listening. But I missed the beginning. Also, I might have wandered off a little bit."

"I thought you were known for your astute detecting skills."

"When I put my mind to it. But I'm a highly selective sleuth. I'm not going to raise my antennae for just any murder."

"Why not? What are your criteria?"

"Well," Nina said, "Ray strikes me as someone just on the edge of sleazy. He might have incurred some gambling debts with the wrong people, or something like that. And quite frankly, sordid little murders like that don't really interest me."

"I didn't realize that you were such a snob. And like most snobs, you're wrong."

There was nothing Nina hated more than being called a snob. She could usually truck out her humble origins and defray the accusation. But in this case, Jonathan was probably right. She was being a snob. "Why do you say that?" she asked.

"Just because the guy was a doorman doesn't mean his murder was routine. You think that only people who have graduate degrees lead interesting lives?"

Like most rich kids, Jonathan had a romance with the proletariat. He hadn't grown up in a crummy neighborhood in the Bronx where nothing interesting ever happened. He had been raised on a street with large trees and large houses where people drank cocktails and cheated on their spouses and occasionally even killed themselves. The Fischmans had lived on the same block for decades and Nina had never heard of even one suicide in the entire neighborhood. "Ray didn't happen to kill himself, did he? Is that a possibility?"

Jonathan shook his head. "No, it didn't sound like it."

"Yeah, I figured." Proved her theory. Guys like Ray were too preoccupied with figuring out how to pay this month's bills. They didn't have the time or energy to contemplate such lofty concepts as ending their life.

"Well, don't be too dismissive of this murder," Jonathan said. "You'll have to take an interest."

"Why is that?"

"Because I'm a suspect."

It was strange, she thought, that in the months she had known him, this was the second time that Jonathan was a suspect in a murder case. Especially since he was exactly the kind of guy who you'd never in a million years think would be mixed up in something like this. That was what she liked best about him, she supposed. He wasn't the kind of person who stirred up a lot of disruptive drama in his life. He saved his Sturm und Drang for his therapist's office. Jonathan always seemed totally happy to be sitting on the couch with her, deciding what movie to go to or when to do a wash. But in a fun, unboring way. It was a calmness that might have made her claustrophobic in the past, but now felt just right. But not right enough to get her to pack her bags.

"So how serious are the police about considering you a suspect?"

"Well, he was shot in my car."

"So I heard. What time did it happen?"

"Soon after eleven. You know, on Thursday morning there's no parking on our side of Eighty-second Street from eight until eleven. So Ray used to double park my car on the other side of the street and then move it back to our side at around eleven. Well, the car was still double parked when they found him."

"Who found him?"

"The traffic cop. One of those horrible Brownies." The Brownies were the most detested group in New York City, the untouchable caste. They buzzed around illegally parked cars like flies around horse dung. They were easily spotted by virtue of their uniforms, which actually were the color of horse dung. "The Brownie was about to write a ticket because the car was double parked after eleven."

"I don't get it," Nina said. "Isn't it illegal to double park at any time?"

"Of course."

"So how come they don't give tickets to illegally parked vehicles all the time? Why wait until eleven? Isn't it just as illegal to double park before eleven as it is after?"

"You won't get a ticket before eleven. That's how things are done in this city. Look, you need to have alternate side of the street parking here, right?"

"Yeah. So that those street sweepers can come along and blow dirt all over your ankles."

"Right," Jonathan said. "But everyone knows that it's physically impossible to park every vehicle in New York City legally. There's just not enough space. You can't even be guaranteed a double parked space during the week. So there's a tacit understanding that it's okay to double park when you can't park on the other side of the street."

"But what about the people who are parked legally? The ones who are blocked in by all the double parked cars? Is this method fair to them?"

"Yes. Because everyone knows that they're going to be blocked in between the hours of eight and eleven if they're parked legally. They shouldn't expect to have access to their cars at that hour. But once eleven o'clock comes, they should be able to move them. That's when it becomes unacceptable to be doubled parked. Which was why the Brownie was giving my car a ticket a little after eleven."

"I see. The law of the jungle."

"Look," Jonathan said, "it's just one of those things. Like traffic signals that say don't walk. Do you pay any attention to them?"

"Well, if it says don't walk, I'll look before I jaywalk."

"Right. That's what don't walk means—look before you jaywalk. And that's what alternate side of the street parking means—time to double park."

"Anyway," Nina said, "the Brownie was writing a ticket when she saw Ray's body in the driver's seat?"

"Yeah. According to the cops, the Brownie was standing in the middle of the street, on the passenger's side. The first thing she noticed was that the button on the passenger door was open. It was only then that she took a closer look and saw that there was a corpse slumped over the steering wheel."

"So whoever shot Ray must have been sitting in the passenger seat."

"I guess so. Since my car has four doors, and it was the front door that was unlocked, he must have been sitting next to Ray. As opposed to hiding in the backseat, or sneaking up and shooting him through the driver's side window. Besides, the cop said that judging by the way the bullet entered Ray's head, the guy was probably sitting next to him."

"Which seemed to imply that the shooter knew Ray. And must have been someone Ray trusted enough to let him into the car."

"Right." Jonathan patted her on the head. "That's my good little sleuth."

Nina had to admit that he had gotten her juices flowing. "And it wasn't you that did it?" she asked.

"Why would I kill Ray? I'd have to be crazy. Do you think I want to spend the rest of my life driving around looking for a parking spot?"

"Where were you between eleven and twelve this morning?"

"In a meeting until a little after eleven. Then in a cab going over to see the Crunchola account people. I must have gotten there at about eleven-thirty. Good enough?"

"So-so. Where are the Crunchola people?"

"Over on Sixth."

"Mm. Not really enough time to swing by and shoot someone on Eighty-second Street, I guess. But alone in a cab is not a great alibi. You didn't happen to notice the driver's name, did you?"

"Are you kidding?"

"Well, even so," Nina said, "you have something else going for you."

"What's that?"

"The unlocked passenger door. Let's say it's eleven o'clock and Ray leaves his post at the door."

"Okay," Jonathan said. "The relief guy comes at eleven so that Ray can go to the bathroom and move his cars. Ray usually moves the cars first so that he doesn't get any tickets. Also all the legal spots for the next day are usually gone by ten after eleven."

"Right. So Ray goes over to your car, unlocks the driver's door and gets in. Before he can turn on the ignition, he sees you coming. What's his immediate instinct? To open the passenger door?"

"I don't know."

"No." Nina was emphatic. "Remember, it's your car. He wouldn't expect you to get in on the passenger side. It's more likely that he'd get out of the car in case you wanted to get into the driver's seat. So it couldn't have been you."

"Thank you."

"Besides, what's your motive?"

"He dinged my fender?"

"Hardly a motive for murder in this town. Besides, it's not as if you're driving a brand-new Lamborghini." Jonathan's car was a mid-eighties Volvo, inherited from his father. "Volvos are supposed to have dings in them. The way tweed jackets are supposed to have patches on the elbows."

"So I'm off the hook?"

"As far as I'm concerned you are. Do you know who did it by any chance?"

"Of course not."

"But maybe you can figure it out."

Jonathan shrugged. "I can't see a reason why anyone would want to kill Ray."

"But wasn't he a money hungry guy?"

"Look, the man lived in an apartment in Jackson Heights and had two little boys and a wife who barely speaks English. She sometimes cleans houses, but mostly she stays home with the kids. Ray wasn't money hungry, he was just trying to make ends meet. Not only did he park cars and get the mail and feed my cat and little stuff like that, but he'd pump gas on the weekend at his brother-in-law's service station in New Jersey. He said that he was saving up to buy his own business."

"What kind of business?"

"A gas station, like his brother-in-law's."

"Maybe," said Nina, "he had borrowed money from some Mafia types. Or was dealing drugs in addition to feeding your cat. Where is your cat, by the way?"

"Hiding from you, no doubt." Nina had been quite taken by the fact that Jonathan had a cat. She thought it was sweet. And rare in a man. She knew a lot of women who had cats, but few men. But then women were always willing to take on another relationship, be it man or beast. Nina had considered Jonathan's cat to be a plus, but to her great chagrin, the cat was insanely jealous of her and hid whenever she came over.

"Where are you, Sasha?" she called. "I'm reaching out to you. Why won't you respond? Where's your sense of sisterhood?" Sasha was a good name for a cat, Nina thought. Although lately people had started using it for children as well. Which wasn't as bad as all those dog names people were sticking their kids with. Like that Kathie Lee Gifford woman, the latest media personality to remind America on a daily basis that you can never be too rich or too thin. The Nancy Reagan of the nineties. She had named her children Cody and Cassidy like a pair of Irish setters.

"Ray wasn't doing anything illegal," Jonathan said.

"How do you know?"

"Would he be bothering to feed Sasha for ten bucks when I went out of town if he was dealing drugs?"

"Take care of the pence and the pounds will take care of themselves. Besides, you did say that he lived in Jackson Heights. Aren't the police always finding pounds and pounds of cocaine in Jackson Heights apartments?"

"Well, he never carried a beeper. And he didn't have that haunted look that someone who owed money to the mob would have. He was a clean guy, trying to get by and hustling a little on the side."

"Wait a minute," said Nina. "When was the last time he fed Sasha?"

"I don't know. Why?"

"When did we go upstate?"

"Around the middle of October. To see the leaves."

"Right. And didn't Ray say that he couldn't feed the cat? I remember because you made such a fuss about her the whole time we were gone. And I kept telling you that the whole idea of having a cat was so that you could leave it alone for a couple of days without worrying. Otherwise you might as well have something substantial. Like a dog or a baby."

"Yeah. So?"

"Didn't you get the impression that he wasn't going to feed the cat anymore?"

"Maybe. He said something about not having the time."

"What do you think that meant?" Nina asked.

"I don't know. Maybe he was busy doing something else."

"Or maybe he was tired of the nickel and dime crap involved in feeding your cat. Sasha had become small potatoes, too small for Ray. He was moving on to something bigger. Something more lucrative. More dangerous."

"Like walking dogs?"

"No, you idiot." She pinched his foot. "Not like walking dogs. Something that got him killed."

"Like what?"

"That's for us to find out."

"So now you're interested? I thought you found Ray too mundane to wonder about why he had been killed. That you confined your curiosity to the haute bourgeoisie."

"You sucked me in."

"It was just a ploy to get your mind off 'Seinfeld.' "

"Well, it worked. But only temporarily." Nina picked up the remote control, smiled sweetly and hit "play."

CHAPTER 3

The "Seinfeld" episode had been a good one, worth the pain of getting thirty minutes less sleep. There was something about the show that made Nina more hopeful about her life. For there she would be, schlepping through the week, by Thursday thinking how trite her life was. "Here I am—still single, still on the Upper West Side, still sitting in coffee shops listening to my friends complain about failed relationships and missed career opportunities and obsessing about whether to terminate psychotherapy. While everyone else has moved on—to motherhood, to assistant vice presidencies, to Chappaqua." And then along comes the "Seinfeld" gang to remind you that your life is indeed hip and funny. And no, it's not true that you might as well be living in the middle of Iowa. And there still is something glamorous about New York coffee shops.

It always perked Nina right up. She noticed that she was at her conversational best on Fridays, infected with a quirky energy that some found annoying but that she thoroughly enjoyed. She had always been impressionable when it came to the media. Nina had spent her entire preadolescence trying to sound like Holden Caulfield. Now she spent her Fridays sounding like George Costanza. She wondered if other women continually overidentified with alienated male losers, or if she was abnormal in this regard. But really, who were you supposed to relate to? Murphy Brown? It was much easier to identify with a guy who wore sweatpants than a woman who owned every single suit that Donna Karan ever manufactured. So when her mother called her at the office on Friday morning, she answered the phone with a whine that was more George than Nina.

"What's wrong?" asked Ida Fischman. "Did I catch you on an intake day?" Nina worked for a federally funded law office that serviced the elderly indigent. Once a week she had to take in new cases, which required listening to much kvetching.

"No, Ma. No intake today. I'm just tired."

"Well, it's no wonder. Every time I talk to you, you're packing up your panty hose and running off to catch the crosstown bus. Why don't you just move in already?" Ida had met Jonathan and liked him. She wasn't one of those mothers who felt that no one was good enough for her daughter. But neither did she worry that her daughter wasn't good enough for anyone. She was a sensible woman, who kept her eyes on the odds and tended to avoid long shots.

"It's not that simple."

"Why not? You want to live with him. He wants you to move in. He's smart, he's cute, he's got a job, he even understands a little Yiddish."

"He happens to be Jewish, except for a little intermarriage a while back."

"That's good enough for me. Besides, he's got a nice apartment in a decent neighborhood. You've got a crummy apartment that you've been wanting to move out of for years. Sounds simple to me."

"For one thing, I don't really like the neighborhood."

"What, it'll kill you to be able to walk to Blooming-dale's?"

"Maybe. Did you ever notice how many anorexic women seem to live in the immediate vicinity of Bloomingdale's?"

"Nina, I think you're getting to the age where you have to worry more about menopause than anorexia."

"You're probably right. Besides, I was never a good candidate. Anorexia is a private school disease. Anyway," Nina continued, "it's not only the neighborhood. It's also the building."

"What's wrong with the building?"

"Too glitzy."

"Nina, complaining about things being too glitzy is a luxury that we in this city can no longer afford. Maybe back when the economy was booming and homelessness meant a few hundred Bowery bums, we could wrinkle up our noses at glitz and look for something with more character. But these days, glitz is good. Glitz is something to aspire to."

"Maybe."

"I'm telling you, doormen are good. Elevators that play Muzak are good. Carpeted hallways are good."

"But the people in the building are creepy. There are all these guys who don't seem to work. They're always walking in and out in the middle of the afternoon carrying tennis racquets. I can't figure out what they do for a living. They all seem to be divorced and go to hair replacement centers. And the women are stewardess types."

"There's no such thing anymore. Have you flown lately?" Ida asked.

"Not as much as you." Her mother, who lived on Social Security and a schoolteacher's pension, seemed to get around quite a bit. She had been to Egypt, China, Indonesia, Alaska and all the rest of the places that had suddenly become de rigueur for retired schoolteachers. It always amused Nina how trendy these women were in their travels. They never paid attention to fashion, or bothered to redecorate their living rooms, but if a cruise on the Inland Passage up to Juneau was where it was at this year, then they were all on board.

"Well, since they won all that litigation about age and weight and pregnancy restrictions, stewardesses look like totally normal people. They have children and stomachs and plain brown hair."

"Then I don't know what the women in Jonathan's building do for a living, but they've clearly never heard of the concept of relaxed fit jeans."

"Nina, you're not moving in with these people. You're just moving in with Jonathan. And I doubt if he wears tight pants."

"God no. He practically invented the concept of relaxed fit. Even his socks are baggy."

"So what's the problem?"

"Ma, it's easy for you to talk. I notice that you don't live in a building where *New York* magazine is considered an intellectual periodical. No, you live on West End Avenue in a building that was built during the Harding administration. Where people subscribe to *The New York Review of Books* and think that contact lenses are only necessary if you work in the theater."

"Look, you know that my living here is a fluke. That if Uncle Irving's client hadn't offered me a rental before the building converted to a co-op, I'd still be pushing my shopping cart up and down Lydig Avenue and taking the IRT home from Lincoln Center. I consider my apartment to be something of a miracle and I don't believe that living on West End Avenue is a God-given right."

"Maybe not. But at least if your doorman was going to go and get himself shot, he'd do it while he was off-duty."

"What are you talking about?"

"Ray the doorman was shot yesterday. Not only that, but he was parking Jonathan's car at the time."

"You mean to tell me that one of the doormen was found dead in Jonathan's car?"

"Right. You see? When you live in a den of iniquity like Jonathan's building, the spillover effect can get you. Now he's bound to be a suspect."

"I don't know if Jonathan's building qualifies as a den of iniquity just because the women wear straight leg jeans. Aren't you turning into quite the prude?" It was a word used liberally in Nina's youth. But now, in this age of sexual epidemics, it ceased to have any meaning. "But tell me what happened."

"Nobody seems to have seen anything. Or know anything about possible suspects or motives."

"Was the doorman a sleazy kind of guy?" Ida asked.

"No, not really. Quick to try and make an extra buck. And Jonathan says that starting around November, he'd become absolutely unctuous, getting oilier as the Christmas season wore on. But he didn't seem desperate or anything."

"Besides, you can't really satisfy a drug habit with extra tips, can you?"

"You're right, Ma."

"Did he used to meet with suspicious characters in the lobby or outside the building?"

"I don't know."

"It's worth finding out. We had a doorman a couple years ago who turned out to be mixed up in some IRA gun-running scandal."

"Was he arrested?"

"No, but he disappeared and no one knew where he

went. It turned out he went underground and later surfaced in Ireland. I found out from the mailman."

"The mailman?"

"Yeah, the letter carrier who has this route. He's an interesting guy, one of those very brilliant types who's so maladjusted that he has to work for the Post Office for the rest of his life."

"You sound like you have a crush on him."

"Well," Ida said, "we've had some very interesting conversations over the years. But he's a little young for me. And he smells and doesn't shave."

"Sounds Hasidic."

"In my day it was the anarchists who didn't shave. The Marxists and the Trotskyites were all clean-shaven. And took baths so that they could relate to the workers."

"So are you one of those old ladies who hangs around the lobby in her housedress, waiting for the mail to come in?"

"We don't wear housedresses anymore. Not since they came out with the tunic top. Such a wonderful invention. Now people like me can shop at the Gap."

"I'm happy for you, Ma." Nina had a small waist, which she felt compelled to show off to compensate for what lay below. It was a curse, really, always looking for fitted tops when everyone else ran around in leggings and sweatshirts. "So do you have a crush on your mailman?"

"Of course not. But I'm telling you, Nina. Those letter carriers know everything that goes on in a building. Who owes money, who has cancer, who's unemployed."

"And how do they know all this?"

"Well, if someone's getting collection notices, or unemployment checks or bills from the oncology department at Mount Sinai, it's not hard to figure out, is it?"

"I guess not."

"Besides, they hear things. And not only about the tenants. They know just as much about the building staff. If you want to find out what happened to Jonathan's doorman, you should ask the mailman."

"I've never even seen the mailman. I don't have the luxury of spending my weekday mornings hanging around waiting for some smelly, hairy postal genius to come by and give me the latest gossip."

"Are you staying at Jonathan's tonight?"

"Probably," Nina said. "He's refused to sleep at my place ever since the living room window stopped closing."

"I see." Nina could tell that on the other end of the line, her mother was shaking her head in despair. And also blaming herself for raising a daughter who didn't have high expectations out of life like window repairs. "Well, tomorrow's Saturday. Take my advice and pay a visit to the mailroom. You might find out something interesting about the deceased. By the way, what was he doing in Jonathan's car?"

"Jonathan used to pay him to move the car when alternate side of the street parking was in effect. So that he wouldn't get a ticket."

"Now what is Jonathan going to do?"

"I don't know. Maybe we'll have to move to the suburbs."

"You know what they say, Nina."

"What's that, Ma?"

"Be careful what you wish for," said Ida Fischman. "You just might get it."

CHAPTER 4

"What time does your mail get in?" Nina asked.

"I don't know," Jonathan said. "Around noon, I guess. Why?"

"I have to talk to your mailman."

"You do? Whatever for?" Jonathan looked up from the *New York Times Magazine*. They were sitting around on Saturday morning waiting to put their clothes in the dryer in the laundry room down the hall.

New Yorkers had a strict hierarchy when it came to laundry access. At the bottom of the ladder were people like Nina, who lived in a building with no laundry facilities and who had to go to Laundromats. The Laundromats were seedy places, filled with people who smoked and ate Ring Dings. The next rung up were residents of buildings who had laundry rooms in the basement. This obviated the need to hang around Laundromats reading discarded copies of the *National Enquirer*, but raised the possibility of being mugged. The next level of desirability included buildings like Jonathan's that had laundry rooms on every floor. Which was an improvement as far as security went. But each laundry room featured only one washer and dryer. So during times like

Saturday morning, the worst of the laundry rush hours, you had to watch your machine like a hawk. Otherwise, someone might sneak in from upstairs and grab the dryer before you had a chance to empty your washing machine.

The luckiest people in the city were the ones who had renovated their co-ops and rewired to permit them to have little stackable units right in their own kitchens. This was rare but not unheard of. This whole laundry syndrome was just another example of how New Yorkers who made a hundred thousand a year lived on the same level as out-of-town residents of trailer parks.

"Now why do you want to talk to my mailman?" Jonathan put down the magazine section and began to play with the little stack of quarters on the coffee table. "Might it have anything to do with Ray's murder?"

"Boy, are you smart."

"You sound surprised."

"You sound offended."

"Well, of course I'm smart," he said. "Since when did you start dating dumb guys?"

Jonathan's use of the word "dating" was just the tiniest bit disappointing, since Nina thought that co-mingling of laundry meant that they were further along than just dating. But she had resolved not to be hypersensitive in this relationship, which was a little bit like Howard Stern resolving not to be sarcastic. You might as well tell the rain not to fall. Besides, hypersensitivity was her stock in trade. If only she could make a living from it.

"I don't date dumb guys. So you agree that the mailman might know something about Ray's murder?"

"Yeah, because I've seen them hanging out together. They seemed to be buddies. But that's the weekday guy I'm talking about. I think there's a different guy on Saturday." Nina had no idea who delivered her mail. But Jonathan had clearly spent enough time between jobs to be able to tell the letter carriers apart. Besides, it took only a couple of minutes to sort out the mail for a small tenement. But in large buildings like Jonathan's, the mailmen usually spent hours in the mailroom. Enough time to become a familiar fixture to the tenants.

"The Saturday guy never hung out with Ray?" she asked.

"I don't know. Why don't you go down and ask him?"

"I will. Right now."

"But first I suggest you put on some appropriate lobby attire." Nina was wearing Jonathan's flannel bathrobe. Which was acceptable for going down the hall to get the laundry, but not for going down to the lobby to get the mail. Saturday morning lobby attire on the Upper East Side was apparently somewhere between hallway attire and shopping at Bloomingdale's attire, between a bathrobe and a leather jacket. Expensive leather jackets seemed to be obligatory for Bloomingdale's on Saturday, no matter what the season.

"Okay, I'll get dressed." She went off to the bedroom to put on last night's pants and sweater.

"Do you want me to come with you?" Jonathan called to her.

"No, you might miss your dryer. I'll be back in a couple of minutes." She reappeared. "Maybe even with bagels." She slipped on Jonathan's leather jacket so that she looked like just another tenant heading down Third Avenue to Fifty-ninth Street to hit a sportswear sale.

The guy she rode down in the elevator with was not wearing a leather jacket, but he was dressed for racquet sports. And he wasn't wearing a toupee, but he did have very evenly spaced plugs of hair that suggested a transplant. And the zipper on his sweat suit was unzipped just enough to reveal chest hair that was distinctly grayer than what had been transplanted. Nina always tried to feel some sympathy for these guys when she saw them going in and out of Jonathan's building, pining away for their kids and their driveways and everything else they'd been divorced from. But they all seemed to be having a good time, rushing from tennis court to poker table. The only time they looked unhappy was on alternate weekends when they had to take Nicole and Brendan to the zoo or the circus or to Grandma's. It was hard to feel sorry for them. In fact, it was hard not to wish she was one of them.

But no matter how hard she tried, she was not going to grow up to be a divorced heterosexual man who used to live on Long Island but now lived on East Eighty-second Street and dated women with the same first names as his daughter's friends. Besides, she had more important things to think about at the moment.

The mailman could have been the one that Ida had described to her. Of course, he wasn't, being that Ida's worked out of 10023, the Ansonia Station, and this one was a Gracie guy out of 10028. But apparently they were of a type. Because this one had a couple days' worth of stubble on his face, lacking the appeal of Mickey Rourke. He also had a ferocious intensity about the eyes, which could easily have connoted some sort of bent brilliance. And now that Nina had gotten closer, yes, there was a subtle odor that Nina recognized from her campus days, a mixture of sweat and printer's ink. Of course, it probably wasn't really printer's ink now, since any maniac who wanted to publish some obscure diatribe of a newsletter was sure to have access to a laser jet printer. Desktop publishing had obviated the need to memorize the California job type case. But printer's ink still had sexy memories for Nina, and she wasn't thoroughly revolted by the stubbly specimen she found boxing the mail.

"Hi there." She flung her hair off her face and tipped her head back to reveal a few extra inches of neck. It was her personal equivalent of crossing her legs, since Nina's neck was her only feature that qualified as long and thin. Nina was always at her confident best when it came to male nerds. Her entire adolescence had been spent attracting and rejecting various members of the audiovisual squad.

This guy wasn't an easy customer, however. "Hello," he said, without taking his eyes off the mail.

Nina tucked her neck back into her sweater and tried a different approach. "They tell me that you know a lot about what goes on here," she said in a "Dragnet" monotone.

"Who's they?" He continued to drop envelopes into mailboxes.

"The local gentry. The men carrying tennis racquets. The women who iron their jeans. The people whose mail you deliver. They say that the letter carrier knows it all." She was speaking nonsense, of course, but she maintained the monotone to give her words authenticity.

She got his attention and he gave her a scrutinizing look. "They're talking about Mundo," he finally answered.

But he mumbled and Nina had a hard time understanding his words. "What's that about a window?" she asked.

"Not a window. Mundo."

"Mundo?" She knew enough Spanish to recognize the word for world. "Like *todo el mundo*?"

"Mundo is the regular. I'm the sub." He seemed to be speaking in some sort of code, so she just patiently waited for him to explain himself. He finally did so, but not before she became uncomfortable enough to begin hopping from one foot to another. "I only deliver the mail here on Saturdays. The rest of the week this guy named Mundo delivers the mail. And that's who they're talking about. Mundo knows everything."

"What kind of a name is Mundo?"

"Well, it's not Ukrainian." The sub shot Nina a snotty yet nerdy look.

"I know it's Spanish, but I never heard it before."

"I think it's short for Edmundo. Or Raimundo."

"Or maybe Desmundo," she added, trying to be helpful and play the game.

"That's a good one. Desmundo." She had clearly gained some respect. "Anyway, Mundo's the one who knows everything. I'm just the sub."

"Oh, I bet you know a few things too," Nina said, doing that thing with her neck again.

This time it worked a little better. He broke into a smile and made full eye contact for the first time. "I guess I know a few things."

"You've undoubtedly heard about Ray the doorman getting killed on Thursday, haven't you?"

"Of course. It was in all the tabloids." He looked like the kind of guy who read four newspapers every day. Plus a dozen obscure magazines each month.

"Well, what do you think? Any theories on who did it?"

"You should talk to Mundo about that." He continued to maintain eye contact, but his lids dropped, giving him a hooded, lizardy look. "They hung out together a lot."

"Mundo and Ray?"

"Yup."

"Would you say that Ray hung out with any shady characters?"

"Yeah. Mundo."

"Really? I don't usually think of letter carriers as shady." Perhaps certifiably insane, she thought, but not shady. In fact, the one thing that federal employees all seemed to have in common was a self-righteous sense of justice that seemed to permeate all agencies from the Post Office to the FBI to the IRS. Pains in the ass, yes, but not shady.

"Well, Mundo has quite a thing going in this building."
You could tell that this guy had been nurturing his own self-righteous sense of justice for many months. He was going to
be easy pickings. Nina didn't even need to trot out her neck.

"What kind of thing?"

"Well, quite honestly, I think he's running a prostitution
ring right here in this building."

"A pimp mailman? It's hard to believe. I mean, I've heard
of people working two jobs, but this is a stretch."

"Why?" The sub seemed offended at her dubiousness.
"It's perfect, don't you see? Mundo gets to stand around the
lobby and talk to all the tenants without arousing any suspicion. Believe me, I've doubled with Mundo during the
Christmas season and have seen what goes on."

"Doubled?" She knew he didn't mean a double date.

"Yeah, when the mail is real heavy the Post Office hires
temps to help out. Sometimes they send a temp out with
Mundo, but sometimes they send me. And I watch. And
listen." He was getting a paranoid look that made Nina consider leaving the room. But in her experience, paranoid people were often perfectly accurate. Her paranoid clients were
always the ones with the best cases.

"And what do you see? And hear?"

"I see a mailman who carries a beeper. Now why would a
postal employee need to carry a beeper? You think anyone
besides me cares whether the mail gets delivered? You
should see what I've seen over the years. Bundles of circu-
lars dropped into trash cans. Postage-due letters that have
been lying around the Post Office since the Carter administration. Parcel post packages that end up in employee lock-
ers."

Nina was sure he was telling the truth. But he was beginning to rant, so she tried to rein him in a bit. "And did you
actually hear Mundo fixing the tenants up with hookers?"

"Well, of course he always spoke softly. And took them off into the far corner of the mailroom when I was around. But what else could it have been? The tenants who came to talk to him were always the same type—the kind of middle-aged guys who wear gold chains. And they couldn't have been talking to him about the mail. I've been subbing in this building for a long time and none of those guys ever have anything to say to me."

"And you said that Ray and Mundo hung out together. Did Ray seem to be involved with this pimping business?"

"Well, he used to let Mundo use the intercom a lot. I mean, I don't know what Mundo gave him in return, but Ray let him do whatever he wanted. The whole thing was shocking, if you ask me."

"And nobody ever did anything about it? The management office or the supervisors at the Post Office?"

"I guess nobody complained."

"But wouldn't it have had some effect on Mundo's ability to deliver the mail? I mean, if he was busy pimping all afternoon, he couldn't have had too much time for his job."

"You don't understand how the Post Office works. When they send you out with the mail in the morning, you get built-in extra time for whatever it is that you want it for. OTB, for example, seems to be a popular spot to spend your double lunch hour." He said it in a way that made clear that he didn't go near the place.

"And what do you do with your extra time?" Nina asked.

"Well, there's a little chess spot over near York that I occasionally frequent. But only after I've finished with all my drops."

"So Mundo had enough time to deliver the mail and pimp for the building. And nobody ever called him on it."

"I would say that's correct."

"And Ray knew about it?"

"Definitely."

"Very interesting. And Mundo will be back on Monday?"

"I would say so."

"I see. You've been very helpful. I'm Nina. What's your name, by the way?"

His eyes widened in a paranoid way that made her regret asking the question. Then he turned his attention back to the mail, so she didn't push it. She had read too many news items about postal workers opening fire on their supervisors. And sometimes even on innocent bystanders in the stamp line. So she let it drop and headed around the corner to the bagel place.

CHAPTER 5

"Did you say pimping?" Jonathan asked.

"I did," Nina said.

"You've got a poppy seed between your teeth."

"Between which teeth?"

"All of them. Actually your teeth are riddled with poppy seeds."

Poppy seed bagels were dangerous. Not only did the seeds get caught between your teeth, ruining whatever effort you'd put into your grooming that day, but they were equally treacherous in the kitchen, liberally coating the counter and the microwave and lurking into eternity inside the toaster. And if Nina had been one of those people who could sacrifice for the sake of appearances, she would give them up forever. But she wasn't, so here she was, digging poppy seeds out from between her teeth.

"How's that?" she asked, offering up her mouth for inspection.

"You missed one." Jonathan dug it out for her. It was sweet having this level of intimacy. She wondered if couples ever got to the point where they picked each other's noses. "So what's all this about pimping?"

"I told you, the Saturday mailman said that Mundo, the guy who delivers the mail during the week, is pimping out of this building. That all those divorced guys you see running around with tennis racquets in the elevator are using Mundo to help them obtain the services of call girls."

"What kind of a name is Mundo?" Jonathan pulled an onion bagel out of the bag and sliced it.

"Well, it's not Ukrainian. Want some tofu spread?" If poppy seed bagels were dangerous, tofu spread was pointless. True, it was low in cholesterol but high in calories. There was no appreciable difference in the fat content of tofu spread and cream cheese. But Nina kept on buying it. Probably just because it was a way of showing some progress, of doing something that your parents never did. Like yuppies who had grown up in Connecticut and now drank vodka instead of gin, which had all these dreadful childhood memories. What gin was to Connecticut, cream cheese was to the Bronx. Although you'd never find that one on the Miller Analogies Test.

"Hit me." Jonathan handed her his bagel for schmearing. "So Mundo the mailman is a pimp?"

"Right. And Ray was a friend of his. The Saturday guy said that Ray used to let Mundo talk to the tenants over the intercom." Nina spread Jonathan's bagel sparingly enough so that he wouldn't get a heart attack, but liberally enough so that he wouldn't get skinny and dump her for a woman who owned her own leather jacket and ironed her nonrelaxed fit jeans.

"So did the Saturday guy think that this had anything to do with Ray's murder?"

"The Saturday guy is a paranoid lunatic. I don't really know what he thinks."

"But you believed him on this pimping business."

"I think I do. Anyway, we should check it out."

"We?"

"Well, you don't have to come. But you'll be missing all the fun."

"When is this fun scheduled to take place?" he asked, right before he tore into his bagel.

"I sort of thought I'd call in late on Monday."

"Call in late. What does that mean? Is that like call in sick?"

"Yeah, except that you show up at some point in the afternoon. After your dental appointment or whatever else you invented."

"I see. And you want me to invent the same dental appointment?"

"It's up to you. If you want to go to work, just leave me the mailbox key so I'll at least look authentic." Nina and Jonathan had gotten to the point where they could pick poppy seeds out of each other's teeth, but they hadn't yet exchanged keys.

"I've got a meeting on Monday morning, so you'll have to venture out on your own." Jonathan's job was still new enough so that he couldn't treat it like an old shoe. Nina, on the other hand, was caught in that syndrome—as soon as you've been at your job long enough to be really good at it, you stop taking it seriously. She wondered if most marriages turned out to have the same problem—as soon as you really understood your spouse, your eyes began to wander.

"Okay. Why don't you give me the key now, so you don't forget."

Jonathan walked slowly over to the hallway table. On the table was a wooden box, inlaid with some mosaic work. The box looked familiar. Nina was sure she had brought a similar one home years ago from somewhere. But whether she had bought it in the Old City of Jerusalem, or the Casbah of Tangier or an open-air market along the Costa Brava, she couldn't say. All the ethnic *chotchkes* of her past, once so treasured, all seemed to blur into a jumble of Eilat stones and Taxco silver. Nina had dumped a lot of that stuff. She was definitely at the point where it was advisable to prune rather than acquire. But she'd make an exception for Jonathan's keys.

He pulled a ring filled with keys out of the box and stared at them for a moment. It was a moment that seemed frozen in time, lasting forever, since Nina was sure he was reassessing their entire relationship in those few seconds. He walked slowly over to her. He had a funny look in his eye, sort of half frightened, half nauseous. "Here," he said, taking forever to hand them to her. "You might as well keep these. The Medeco is for the top lock. The little square one is the mailbox."

"You sure you want me to keep them all? I only need the mailbox key." And I don't want you to think I manipulated you into this, she added silently. Because then you'll resent me forever, if I'm lucky. If I'm not, you'll take them back and leave. And there I'll be, back at B'nai Jeshurun potlucks and the Bar subcommittee cocktail parties, looking for men and meeting more women.

And she knew she'd miss him. She'd miss the way he always wore those stupid shirts with the sleeves rolled all the way down and the way he'd wait to get a haircut until he looked like a Yorkshire terrier without a barrette.

Besides, she'd miss the sex. Because maybe Jonathan wasn't one of those dynamic go-getters who was always running off to catch the next business opportunity. But there was one thing Jonathan had proved about guys who weren't in a hurry. And that was that being in a rush might pay off in most places, but not in the bedroom.

But then, she argued with herself, if you're so intent on holding on to this guy, why don't you just move into his apartment already? Because, she answered, I want to get to be the ambivalent one.

"No, no." Jonathan pressed the keys into her hand. "I want you to have them." He looked less nauseous by now.

"Okay. Thanks. Maybe I'll stay over Sunday night and take the morning off. Then after I take a look at Mundo, I'll head over to the office."

"And what do you expect to see?"

"Some mailman having furtive conversations in the corner of the mailroom with middle-aged male tenants."

"But even if that is what you see," Jonathan said, "how do you know what's really going on? Mundo could be into all sorts of things besides pimping."

"Such as?"

"Running numbers."

"Middle-class white guys don't play the numbers."

"Well, he could be some sort of bookie."

"Do they still have bookies? Since OTB?" she asked.

"OTB is just for horse racing. Bookies take bets on other sports, like boxing, football, stuff like that."

"So maybe he is a bookie. I would think that the same kind of guys who use hookers probably bet on college basketball, wouldn't you?"

"Probably," Jonathan said. "You should also consider the possibility that Mundo is into dealing some sort of controlled substance."

"I don't know. The guys in this building look like their drug of choice is take-out Chinese food."

"Well, maybe he gets them cleaning ladies."

"Puh-leeze." Nina rolled her eyes. "Even if Mundo was supplying the entire building with illegal-alien cleaning ladies, how many conversations would that entail? I mean, you set something up with the woman on a weekly basis and then if she runs off with the silver or drinks up the half gallon of Scotch in one afternoon, then you fire her and go down and see Mundo again. How often does that happen? With hookers it's a different story. You don't give them the key to your apartment and tell them to come every Tuesday."

"I guess some guys do."

"Yeah, but isn't it more like a 'I've got the urge, I think I'll make a call' kind of thing?"

"I don't know," Jonathan said. "You seem to be the expert."

"Besides, the Saturday guy said that Mundo carried a beeper. Do you need a beeper to dispatch cleaning ladies?"

"Okay, okay, you've made your point. It's not cleaning ladies."

"But you're right about the bookie thing. It might not be so easy to figure out what's going on just by watching. I'm going to have to eavesdrop."

"Nina, I'm sure you're up to the challenge."

"It is something I'm good at, although my lip-reading skills could stand some improvement."

"Anyway, the laundry's done. What do you want to do this afternoon? Go to the movies?"

Going to the movies with men was something Nina tried to avoid. They rarely wanted to see the films on her list, things that featured over-the-hill British actresses running around gardens in Tuscany. Merchant and Ivory had helped bridge the gap somewhat, so that even regular guys who drove American cars and drank domestic beer could be convinced to take an occasional look at an Italian villa. But most of the time, no matter how evolved they were, they'd rather see a motorcycle crash through a plate-glass window. And it was easier to sneak off to see Joan Plowright on a Tuesday

night by yourself or with a girlfriend than waste time argu-
ing with some man.

Jonathan was better than most. Maybe it was his art
school background that had given him decent taste, androgynous without being effeminate. Nina had been won over
when she found out that he had actually gone to see both
the Matisse retrospective at the Modern and *Like Water for
Chocolate* on his own. Although she had caught him watching a televised broadcast of James Bond's *Octopussy* the other
night.

"Nah, I'm not really in the mood for a movie," she said.

"What do you want to do instead?" he asked.

"Nothing."

"You want to do nothing?"

"Yeah, isn't that the point of being in a relationship?" she
said.

"What's that?"

"That you get to sit around and do nothing."

"Sounds good to me." He put his feet up on the coffee
table and picked up the *Times Magazine* again, while Nina
just sat there, fingering Jonathan's keys.

She would have to practice her lip-reading for Monday,
she thought. And maybe dress up so that she wouldn't
arouse suspicion. Make herself look inconspicuous. Like an
old lady, she thought. There's no one as invisible in Manhattan as an old lady. Nobody wants to acknowledge her exis-
tence. Everyone's afraid to make eye contact for fear she'll
end up wanting something from them. Nina could borrow
some clothes from her mother. Support hose and such. Or
better yet, maybe she'd ask her mother to come over and
hang around the mailroom to eavesdrop on Mundo. Why
fabricate when you could get the real thing? Now that Ida
Fischman was retired, she was always up for a Monday af-

ternoon adventure. Something like this might even get her over to the East Side.

"I'm going to make a call," she said, and slipped off to the bedroom.

CHAPTER 6

"Nice rug," Ida Fischman said.

"I guess I never really noticed." Nina looked at Jonathan's rug as if for the first time. It was red, with an intricate black pattern throughout.

"It's a Bokhara, isn't it?"

"I wouldn't know." Nina's mother often surprised her. Ida was supposed to be the antithesis of materialism, one of those women who had been involved in leftist politics in Hunter College before the war and who had stayed in the boroughs and worked and raised children and never had the time or resources for fashion or interior decoration. The Fischmans' budget, which always remained modest, went primarily for the experiential as opposed to the material. Everybody in the family wore hand-me-downs, but there was always money for summer camp. And even though the living room furniture was secondhand as well, school vacations were spent at some culturally enriching spot like the Smithsonian Institution or Williamsburg, Virginia.

So it continually caught Nina off-guard when her mother started chatting like one of those ladies who hang around Sotheby's. This syndrome had become more pronounced since the death of Nina's father. Who, Nina now suspected, had been the real antimaterialist force in the family. It was entirely possible that Ida could have been perfectly happy lunching in the trustees' dining room at the Metropolitan Museum of Art and going for fittings at her dressmaker's instead of teaching in the New York City public schools and trying things on in the aisles of Alexander's. Everyone used the aisles back then, before the Farkas family had seen fit to install more than two fitting rooms per selling floor.

These days, when you least expected it, Ida Fischman, who wore New Balance running shoes and carried a canvas Channel Thirteen tote bag, would casually toss off a bit of knowledge that was a window into a world of hand-painted silk upholstery and Hermès scarves and Kelly bags. Nina didn't know anything about rugs, never having had the need to purchase one. And maybe being able to spot a Bokhara was nothing much, something everyone and their aunt Ethel could do. But it made Nina nervous, wondering what other desires her mother had suppressed during her life. And inevitably wondering whether Nina herself was re-enacting a lifetime of suppression, not even aware of her secret lusts for silk bathrobes and Chippendale chairs.

"It's definitely a Bokhara," Ida said. "And a nice one. An antique."

"Now why would somebody want to buy a used rug?" Nina hoped that her mother knew she was kidding.

"You know, you could be very happy in this apartment. Even if the mailman is a pimp."

"Yeah, well, maybe. We'll see what happens. In the meantime, I think we should set out some game plan."

"What's the big deal?" Ida waved dismissively. "I put on my house slippers, loiter in the mailroom and eavesdrop on the mailman's conversation. Easiest thing in the world. I do it every day."

"So the truth comes out. You actually spend your days in house slippers. While I thought you were taking courses and seeing matinees and going to the shrink."

"I do all those things as well. But I still have time to loiter in the mailroom. After all, the shrink is down to weekly. Even I can't stand to listen to myself whine about something my mother did back in 1927 more often than once a week. And I don't go to the theater as much as I used to. For the prices they charge you could hire someone to come and read the lines to you in your own apartment."

"Well, where are we going to get house slippers from? I don't think that Jonathan has any."

"I brought my own." Ida triumphantly pulled a cracked pair of pink mules out from her Channel Thirteen tote bag.

"Ma, how old are those things?"

"No older than you. Just wait, with the right pair of floppy socks they'll create the perfect effect."

"How can someone who is able to identify an antique Bokhara still wear those on her feet?"

"I'm a complicated woman."

"You must be, to spend all those decades in psychotherapy. You know, long-term analysis is very passé. Short-term crisis intervention has taken its place."

Ida shrugged. "So call me old-fashioned."

"Anyway, what I think we should do is go down to the lobby and then split up. I'll sit down and pretend I'm waiting for someone while you go into the mailroom and loiter."

"Okay."

"There's just one thing I'm worried about," Nina said.

"What's that?"

"This is a pretty glitzy building. I've never seen any old ladies here. You might stick out like a sore thumb."

"Don't worry. There are a few in every building in Manhattan. Like cockroaches. You don't see them except at mail time. Trust me. I'm familiar with the habits of my people."

Nina shrugged. "You're the alter kocker anthropologist. Let's go."

"Just let me put on my socks and slippers and we're off." Ida removed her New Balance running shoes and replaced her white sweat socks with a stretched-out pair of pilled Ban-Lons, which must have been as old as the slippers. Combined with Ida's loose brown corduroy jumper, the effect was perfect. She looked exactly like the kind of old lady you avoid like the plague, for fear that she'll start telling you about her nephew the cardiologist and you'll never escape.

The mail was already being sorted when they got to the mailroom. And Ida was right, there were two old ladies in baggy clothes, hanging around waiting for the mailman to finish. He was a very short Hispanic guy wearing the blue-gray uniform of the Post Office. The building was large enough to have a truck drop off the sacks of mail before the letter carrier even got there, so the mailman did not need a cart.

"That must be Mundo, don't you think?" Nina asked her mother as they peeked into the mailroom's entrance.

"I would think so."

"Ma, what if one of the old ladies spots you as an impostor? After all, they must all know each other."

"Don't worry. I'll say that I'm visiting my son for a few days and I thought I'd come down and get his mail."

"But that sounds ridiculous."

"It sounds ridiculous to you, but it won't sound ridiculous to them. I'm sure they'd do the same under similar circumstances. Hanging around waiting for the mail is something old ladies do by force of habit, even if they're in a strange building."

"All right. Here's the key. Remember, it's Fourteen E. So

you should actually get the mail after he puts it in, for the sake of authenticity.''

"Fine. And I see there's a bulletin board in the mailroom, which will give me something to do while I'm loitering. It's always good to have a prop.''

"Good luck. I'll be on the couch in the lobby. Come get me when you're through.''

Nina had brought something to read while she waited. That was something her mother the schoolteacher had taught her to do and she had never abandoned the habit. Through the years, no matter how crazy her life had gotten, no matter which drug she was under the influence of, she always had something to read. Right now she had one of those back issues of *The New Yorker* that plagued her constantly. She was always carrying one around, intent on finishing some article by Oliver Sachs on autism or even a twenty-pager on the political situation in Central America if she was particularly ambitious. But everything besides the fiction, "The Talk of the Town" and the cartoons seemed like homework. And she was rarely any more successful with the essays than she had been with geometry.

She was staring at a vodka ad when Ida appeared, giving her the thumbs-up sign with one hand and clutching Jonathan's mail with the other. As soon as they were in the elevator, Nina gave his mail the once-over. Not that she wasn't curious about Mundo, but a stack of mail was as irresistible as an open medicine cabinet.

"Nosy, nosy," Ida said.

Nina ignored her. When she had assured herself that Jonathan wasn't receiving any postcards from women in St. Tropez, she turned her attention back to her mother.

"Nobody questioned me. That was a piece of cake," Ida said as they reentered the apartment. "Except that I almost broke my neck when one of my socks got caught under my slipper."

"An occupational hazard of being a snoop. So what's the story?"

"Exactly what the Saturday guy told you. There was a steady stream of middle-aged guys in and out of the mailroom. What's with these men? What are they doing running around in sweat suits in the middle of a weekday? Don't they work?"

"I can't figure it out either," Nina said. "They're like Kramer on 'Seinfeld.' Professional hangers-around."

"Anyway, they were all having these private conversations with Mundo. Which weren't all that difficult to overhear. Even for an old lady with some hearing loss in the upper decibel range."

"And is he pimping?"

"Without a doubt. The tenant would supply Mundo with the time and place and Mundo would respond with the girl's name."

"Did they discuss price?"

"Mostly Mundo would just say that the fee was as usual and the other guy would nod. Once he mentioned the sum of three hundred dollars. Pretty good money, huh?"

"Not really, when you realize that some people get that for cutting your hair."

"Not for cutting my hair." Ida fingered her plain gray bob. "I won't pay more than fifteen."

"Fifteen? Jesus, Ma, people pay a hundred just to get their poodle clipped these days. Anyway, did Ray's name come up?"

"No. Just the girls."

"Did they all have names like Taffy and Bambi?"

"No, I guess that's an untrue stereotype. Actually, one of them was named Dolores."

"I can't imagine going to a hooker named Dolores. It means pain in Spanish."

"Maybe she's into whips," Ida said.

"Well, I wonder if this had anything to do with Ray's murder. I'd love to talk to Mundo myself, but I'm sure he wouldn't be forthcoming with me."

"Why don't you get Jonathan to talk to him?"

"About what?"

"You know. Pretend he's in need of Mundo's services. Then maybe he'll be able to get something out of him. Do you think Jonathan would do that?"

"Maybe. But how should he approach him? Just walk right up to him in the mailroom and say 'Excuse me, could you help me to have a good time?' And then say 'Hey, how about those Mets? And how about that murder?' "

"Look, Jonathan's an intelligent person."

Nina felt good when her mother said that. She knew it was infantile, that all those years of therapy should have helped her to separate, to break her addiction to her mother's approval. But it made her feel good anyway. "And on what are you basing that judgment?"

"Anyone who subscribes to the *Atlantic Monthly* can't be too stupid."

"And you accused me of being nosy."

"Well, you can't really miss the cover of a magazine. It's not like I read every return address, the way you did."

"Anyway," Nina said, "he is intelligent. So what's your point?"

"He can feel out the situation and see if there's anything to be gleaned from it. It might be the only entree you'll get."

"It just might be. Besides, he's the one who should be investigating this murder. It's his beloved doorman who was shot down in cold blood in Jonathan's very own car."

"Does he have an alibi?" Ida asked.

"Yeah. Not a hundred percent airtight, but it'll do."

"Well, that's fortunate." Ida shot Nina a sharp look. Sharp enough to remind her daughter that the murderer of Nina's childhood friend had been a sexy Irish hunk who Nina had seen fit to take into her bed.

"Patrick was a mistake, Ma. One that I wouldn't make again."

"I know. Although I can't say much for that pothead lawyer you took up with afterward."

"Tom was another mistake. Jonathan's different. For one thing, he's Jewish. Mostly Jewish, anyway. You should be thrilled."

"I'm thrilled, I'm thrilled. And he has excellent taste," Ida added.

"Thank you," Nina said.

"I was talking about the Bokhara. But you're not bad either."

CHAPTER 7

"**This is ridiculous,**" Jonathan said. "**I can't believe I'm** doing this."

"Go on. It'll be fine. I'll be in the lobby, waiting for you. On the couch. And take your time, I brought something to read." Nina nudged him out of the elevator with her copy of *The New Yorker*.

"But I don't know how to phrase it. Besides, do I look like a john to you?"

"As a matter of fact, you don't. Which is why I hang around with you."

Jonathan seemed slightly offended. "I can look sleazy if I try," he insisted. He let his lower lip hang down in that adenoidal way of a Bronx teenager in the fifties.

"Sorry," she said, "that won't do it. You'd have to give up those cotton shirts you always wear and put on something with a shine. And roll up the sleeves and open a couple of buttons."

Jonathan shook his head. "No, not while my mother's still alive."

"I see where your allegiances lie." Nina had yet to meet the woman. When the day came she'd have to remember to wear something without synthetic content. She wondered when that day might be. Both of them were avoiding it, albeit for different reasons.

Nina kept putting it off because she doubted whether anything good could come of it. The way Jonathan described his mother, she sounded like the kind of woman who judged people on things like table manners and whether they wore black with navy. And she didn't sound like someone who would bother to look past anyone's black and navy to see the inner beauty of their soul. Nina knew enough not to wear black with navy, but could not be counted on to not talk with her mouth full, no matter how hard she tried.

Nina wasn't quite sure why Jonathan was avoiding introducing her to his mother. It was probably a combination of complicated and neurotic reasons. Undoubtedly a smattering of "I fall apart around my mother and I don't want Nina to see me that way" along with a soupçon of "I don't want my mother to think I can't get someone who doesn't talk with her mouth full" and a dash of "Who needs the dread and anxiety of not knowing what will happen; it's easier to put the whole thing off and avoid a migraine."

"Do you want to discuss my mother?" he said. "Or do you want to help me figure out what I should say to Mundo. Because if it's my mother you're interested in, I can go on for a couple of hours a week for at least a decade. That much I've proven."

"We'll do your mother some other time. But we practiced this Mundo thing already. Just follow the script we wrote."

"Yeah, but what if Mundo doesn't know his lines? I mean, it's one thing to approach Nina Fischman in my living room to hook me up with a call girl. It's another thing to ask my mailman."

"Everybody else does it. You said yourself that you've seen that guy Howie from down the hall talking to Mundo in the mailroom. If Howie can do it, you can. Don't you have any experience in these matters?"

"Would you prefer that I had?"

"Well, no, not really. But at this particular time, it could come in handy."

Jonathan shrugged and hesitated at the door to the mailroom. Mundo was there, pulling bundles of mail out of the sacks that lay in the corner of the room. "Now go ahead." Nina gave Jonathan a little push in Mundo's direction. Unfortunately, at the precise moment that Nina's hand made contact with Jonathan's shoulder, Mundo looked up at them. She beat a hasty retreat to the lobby, but was sure that they had blown it. Would you fix a man up with a hooker if his girlfriend had just pushed him toward you? It might look a little bit suspicious.

She sat down on the couch and had hardly even started "The Talk of the Town" when Jonathan ambled over, looking defeated. "Forget it," he said, sitting down next to her. "I think you messed up the whole thing by pushing me while he was watching."

"What happened?"

"He just laughed at me. He asked if I had my mother's permission. It was humiliating."

"Did you say it the way we rehearsed it?"

"Yeah, I did. I said exactly what I was supposed to say. That a friend of mine in the building suggested that Mundo could be helpful in widening my social circles."

"And what did he say?"

"That's when he laughed and asked for a note from my mother. He obviously saw you pushing me."

"Is it possible that he really thought I was your mother?" Nina was horrified. She had spent her whole life worrying about being fat, so it had never occurred to her to worry about looking old.

"I'm sure he didn't think you were my mother. But you shouldn't have pushed me. Why didn't you just drag me over to him by my ear, for Godssakes?"

"What else did he say?"

"That he was sure that I was a big boy and could take care of myself. That I didn't need anyone helping me to widen my social circles. Then he just turned back to the mail and ignored me."

"Oh no." Nina folded and refolded a corner of her magazine. "What do we do now?"

"You know something?"

"What?"

"He doesn't really look like a pimp, does he?"

"And what do pimps look like?" she asked. "I thought you had no experience in these matters."

"Well, there are those pimps in the movies, the black guys with the big hats and the magenta Lincoln Town cars. And then there's Sydney Biddle Barrows."

"She wasn't a pimp. She was a madam."

"What's the difference, really? Other than gender?"

"I don't know," Nina said. "I don't know anything about the business of prostitution. I mean, our generation did it for free. You think all these guys that got it for nothing in college are willing to pay for it later on? I can't imagine it. How do all these whorehouses stay in business anyway?"

"I guess there was a substantial portion of the population that did not attend the State University of New York."

"Don't tell me that the boys you went to school with had to pay for it."

"I went to art school. They had each other."

Which raised all sort of questions in Nina's mind that were more troubling than whether or not Jonathan had ever frequented hookers. Actually, frequenting hookers in this day and age could be reassuring. But Jonathan seemed heterosexual and had a short early marriage to a hot Italian aerobics instructor to prove it. So Nina decided to leave well enough alone and probe no more along those lines.

"What is it about Mundo that makes him not look like a pimp?" she asked.

"He's so short."

"But that's classic, isn't it? A man who feels inadequate about his height commandeering the sex lives of dozens of women. You see it in court all the time."

"You see short pimps in court?".

"No, not short pimps. I'm talking about SJL syndrome."

"SJL. Let me guess." Jonathan paused. "Single Jewish Losers?"

"Close. Short Jewish Litigators. They're so bossy and arrogant. Real pains." She knew she had the female equivalent, of course. CJW syndrome. Chubby Jewish women who knew they had to be twice as smart, twice as articulate and talk twice as fast and long to compensate for their figures. You saw them on "Jeopardy!" all the time, ringing in first. In her heart Nina knew that if she had been born thin, her personality could be entirely different. Laconic, or something along those lines.

Since she was a victim of CJW syndrome, she should have a little *rachmones* for the SJLs. But those guys were so difficult to negotiate with, it was hard to be sympathetic.

"Well, I don't think that Mundo's height is determinative of whether or not he's pimping," Nina said. "Besides, he didn't deny it. Just brushed you off."

"So what do you want to do next? I'm not going to try and talk to him again. I've taken enough time off from work already. And my boss is coming back from L.A. tomorrow and I really should go into the office for a couple of hours this afternoon."

"Okay, I'm not going to force you. Maybe we can talk to your friend Howie."

"He's not my friend. Have you ever seen him?"

"No."

"He wears a gold chain. My friends don't wear gold chains."

"All right, your neighbor Howie. What's his last name? Do you know?"

"Mandel."

"Are you kidding? Like the comedian?"

"Yeah. Look, it's not that strange. Back in the fifties, when there were all these baby boy Mandels being born, it must have occurred to more than one Mrs. Mandel to name her newborn Howard. I'm sure there are also several Howard Sterns running around the greater metropolitan area."

"Maybe. I once knew a lawyer named Roy Cohn, but he changed his name."

"I don't blame him."

"Anyway," said Nina, "let's ask your neighbor Howie out for a drink tonight. Then we'll get him to come clean about Mundo and see if he thinks that Ray was involved in this pimping business."

"Okay."

"Should we call him now? Do you think that he's home?"

"He might be. He's often around during the day."

"What does he do for a living?"

"He works in his uncle's export business. I know that he has to go overseas sometimes. But when I was unemployed, I used to see him hanging around a lot."

"Let me guess. With a tennis racquet."

"No, Howie's more of a jogger than a tennis player."

"And he's divorced?"

"Yup."

"How did I guess?"

"Nina, don't forget that I'm also divorced. And that I have occasionally been seen on a Tuesday afternoon heading down in the elevator with a tennis racquet. Should I be lucky enough to be invited to play."

It made Nina think of all the women in Manhattan who had tennis club memberships or parents with clay courts. Women who would be glad to bring Jonathan home with them and introduce their mothers to their new Jewish boyfriend. Even if he did collect unemployment for a while last year.

"Well, that shut me up," she said. "Which, as you know, is no mean feat." She felt bad, but the urge to stereotype had always been strong for Nina. Up there with eating ice cream when it was already in your freezer. A shrink had once told her that whenever she found herself in the middle of a sentence that contained the words "one of those" she should immediately stop talking.

"Don't feel bad. I know you mean well," he said. "It's just that you don't realize when you're being offensive."

When you've spent your childhood not having anyone notice you, being offensive wasn't something you usually felt you had to monitor for. But that was no excuse. "I'm sorry."

"It's okay. Look, do you want to go upstairs and call Howie? Maybe he's around. Although I don't know what good all this is really going to do. I mean, even if Howie confirms that Mundo is the mailman pimp and that Ray knew about it and used to cooperate. Even if he tells us that Mundo was cutting Ray in on the action. What is that going to prove about Ray's murder?"

"Don't you think that finding out that a murder victim is a partner in a pimping operation can be somewhat illuminating?" she asked. "Don't you think it might lead to some clue as to who killed him? Or do you think that it's immaterial, just a silly little coincidence?''

"I guess you're right. But, Nina?''

"What?''

"Why are we trying to solve this murder anyway?''

"For Chrissakes, Jonathan. That man was shot in your car. The validity of your alibi depends on a cabdriver whose name you don't know. Aren't you a little bit curious as to who did it?''

"Not as curious as you are, I guess.''

"You don't make as good a sleuthing partner as my mother, that much is clear. I mean, one phone call and the woman was crosstown like a shot, clutching her house slippers and her synthetic socks. And you—it's too much trouble for you to take your neighbor out for a drink.''

"Please don't hock me about this anymore. I'll take Howie out for a drink. I'll have him in for a drink. I'll even make him dinner, if that's what you want. I'll iron his shirts, give him a foot massage, stand in line at the Motor Vehicle Bureau to get his license renewed. But I really don't want to take any more time off from work.''

"I promise you won't have to. If there's any dangerous weekday sleuthing to be done, I'll take my mother along for protection. Now let's go upstairs and call Howie Mandel.''

CHAPTER 8

Howie Mandel looked kind of like the other Howie Mandel, an overgrown kid in sneakers and a Mets jacket. It was hard to imagine that he was the father of two sons. But on his bookcase sat a photo of two little boys also wearing sneakers and Mets jackets. They looked like mini-Howies and, according to their father, were named Jason and Jeffrey and lived with their mother in Plainview, Long Island.

Howie had been home when Jonathan called. Nina was starting to think that this business of everyone in New York City working all the time was a myth. Maybe it had been true during the eighties, when there was money to be made around the clock. But lately it seemed that Manhattan apartment buildings were stacked with people watching Oprah. Howie had suggested going out for a beer on the spot, but Jonathan insisted that he had to at least drop by the office that afternoon. So the engagement was put off until that evening. Howie Mandel clearly did not have a demanding social calendar.

He took them over to a bar on Second Avenue, the sort of place that the tabloid press refers to as a watering hole. It was frequented by the kind of yuppies who didn't have graduate degrees. The young kind, more likely to be Met than Yankee fans. The baby boomers born late in the fifties, after the National League teams had already moved to California and their parents had moved out of the boroughs.

Since it wasn't quite baseball season, the Knicks instead of the Mets were playing on the television above the bar. Howie gave the TV a quick glance, greeted the bartender and then led Jonathan and Nina to the back. "My regular table," he explained, pointing to one in the corner.

"So you come here all the time?" asked Nina.

"Yeah. I like the mozzarella sticks," and ordered a plateful along with a round of beers.

Mozzarella sticks were more evil than the devil himself. Cheese was bad enough, but fried cheese was in a league of its own. Nina's heart always soared whenever anybody ordered them, since she never had the nerve to do so.

"Mozzarella sticks, huh?" she said. "You're my kind of guy. What other vices do you indulge in?"

Howie laughed. "Good lead-in. Jonathan said you wanted to know about Mundo." That was the good thing about Mets fans. Maybe they didn't have graduate degrees, or go to the theater, or weren't old enough to remember Simon and Garfunkel's early albums. But they also weren't pretentious and they didn't beat around the bush. She could tell that Howie wasn't going to pretend that he didn't know what they were talking about.

"Yeah, we want to know what the story is with the mailman," she said. "We hear he's a pimp. Is that true?"

"Yup. Convenient, isn't it? Not only that, but most of his girls live in the building."

"You're kidding," Jonathan said. "I never knew."

"How long you been living in your place?" Howie asked him.

"Six years."

"Hah. And you thought they were really stewardesses, didn't you?"

"But I've seen them in their uniforms."

"Well, I guess there are some legitimate stewardesses in the building. But some of them are moonlighting."

"Really?"

"Really. The kind of girl that Mundo sends you, they're not the street hooker kind. Not your desperate drug addict types. They're pretty normal, actually. A lot of them are from out of town, trying to make it as actresses and models."

"Why don't they wait on tables, like they're supposed to?" Nina said.

"Have you ever waited on tables?" Jonathan asked her.

"Me? No, I'd be a disaster." Nina had performed a string of blue collar jobs in the seventies, when feminism still had denim overtones. But somehow it had seemed less scary to drive a yellow cab in New York than to risk spilling hot chili all over a customer's lap. "I knew enough to steer clear of that."

"If you didn't want to do it, why should they?"

"Right," said Howie. "I guess they want to make as much money in as little time as possible. They're not interested in slinging hash in some grimy joint and living in a walk-up in Hell's Kitchen."

"You mean they're not willing to sacrifice for their art."

"I mean they're just like you and me. They want air conditioning and cable and a doorman."

"So you've availed yourself of Mundo's services?" she asked Howie.

"Occasionally." He didn't seem upset by the question.

"But I don't get it. All I know are single women who are dying for someone to sleep with. Why pay for it?"

"Spending a coupla hours with one of Mundo's girls is a

lot different than spending an evening with one of *your* friends."

"My friends? What do you mean?"

He smiled at her in a knowing way that made her feel condescended to. "No offense, but I know the kind of women you're talking about. First I'd have to listen to her complain about her job, then obsess about whether or not to quit therapy, then cross-examine me about my divorce."

She decided it would be too distracting to get offended. "Sounds like our first date, doesn't it, Jonathan?"

"It's easier," Howie continued, "to cough up a couple of hundred bucks to Mundo and spend my time listening to some twenty-two-year-old with long hair tell me what a stud I am."

"I guess I can't argue with that," Nina said. "You make it sound so good, I'm ready to try it myself. The next time one of my friends wants to order in Chinese food and whine about her life, I'll just tell her 'Sorry, I'm going to see Dolores instead.' "

"How do you know about Dolores?" Howie looked genuinely surprised.

"Eavesdropping."

"Very good."

"But don't you worry about disease?" she asked.

"So you put on a condom. What's the big deal?"

It was true. It wasn't a big deal for men. It was a lot easier to put on a condom than try to convince someone else to put one on.

"You know," Nina said, "I sent Jonathan over to talk to Mundo to see what was going on down there. Jonathan told him that he had heard that Mundo could help him widen his social circles."

"And what did Mundo say?"

"He just brushed me off," Jonathan said. "Didn't acknowledge anything."

"I figured as much," Howie said.

"How come?"

"You've got to have someone introduce you. Someone he trusts. I mean, it's not like he's open for business to the public. He's a federal employee engaging in illegal activity. On the government's time, no less. Whaddya expect, that he's going to welcome you and hand you a schedule of rates?"

"And I guess the fact that I practically pushed you into the mailroom didn't help matters," Nina said.

"Yeah, that probably wasn't so cool."

"Sorry."

"So what's the deal?" Howie asked. "Where is all this leading? I assume you didn't push Jonathan toward Mundo because you wanted to get him laid."

"No, I don't like to contract out that particular activity. Now, cleaning the house is another matter. Anyway, we got caught up in this because of Ray the doorman. As you must have heard by now, he was parking Jonathan's car at the time of his murder."

"Right, I heard. No one's accusing you of being involved in the shooting, are they, Jon?"

"So far they don't seem to be. But you never know, I guess."

"What about a conspiracy theory?"

It used to be a fancy word, one that a guy like Howie wouldn't use. But since Oliver Stone made that *JFK* movie, everyone had starting throwing it around with reckless abandon.

"Well," said Jonathan, "I don't have a motive. Why would I conspire to murder my doorman?"

"You said he used to feed your cat when you went out of

town. Maybe he saw something in your apartment that he wasn't supposed to see."

"Thanks a lot. I was going to pick up the tab, but if you're just gonna sit around and come up with theories about my guilt . . . well, I have half a mind to cancel the mozzarella sticks. But I wouldn't want to break Nina's heart."

"Yeah, where are those sticks?" She looked around for the waitress.

"Personally, I could use my beer. Right away," said Jonathan.

"Now, don't get nervous," she said. "He's just playing with you. Right, Howie?"

"Mmmm." Howie drummed his fingers on the table. Nina tried to figure out if he was nervously suspicious of Jonathan, or just the kind of guy who still played "Wipe-Out" whenever the conversation lagged.

"Right, Howie?" she repeated.

"Sure," he said. "But what makes you think that Mundo had anything to do with what happened to Ray?"

"Doesn't it seem suspicious to you? A mailman who pimps and a doorman who lets him use the intercom to talk to the tenants?"

"Yeah, Mundo called me on the intercom once. I told him to get a mobile phone, but he stuck with his beeper. Those Spanish guys really love their beepers."

"Jonathan has a mobile phone," Nina said. "And I must say, it's a big convenience. But you don't exactly look cool, standing in the middle of the street, with your little antenna up. You look like . . . well . . ."

"An asshole," Howie suggested.

"Yeah, an asshole," Nina said. "Beepers are much cooler." The waitress came by with their beers and a plate of healthy-looking mozzarella sticks, the size of cigars.

"So what do you think the deal was between Ray and Mundo?" Jonathan asked. "Was he cutting him in?"

"Just for letting him use the intercom? I doubt it. No, I never heard them discussing anything that sounded like business. I think that they just hung out together a little, you know?"

"Like how much?"

"I don't know."

"Did they sit around and play dominoes together? Or did they just shoot the shit a bit while on the job?"

"Uh, Nina, I think that the domino thing might be offensive," Jonathan said. "I don't think that all Hispanic men sit around and play dominoes. The way that not all Jewish women sit around and play mah-jongg."

"Well, if you're going to get p.c. on me, I feel compelled to inform you that Hispanic is no longer acceptable. The preferred term is Latino."

"I thought that was out."

"It was out. Now it's not."

"Anyway," Howie interjected, "I never saw them playing dominoes. But they wouldn't exactly set up a table, break out the rum and Coke and turn up the boom box in the lobby, would they now?"

"Nina, see what you started with the dominoes?"

"Sorry. But, Howie, did they seem close? Or did they just have a professional building-employee demeanor? Did they just nod at whatever the lobby equivalent of the water cooler is? Or was it more than that?"

"I assume it was more than that if Ray was letting him use the intercom to conduct business."

"Was it only Ray who let him use the intercom?"

"Well, Ray was on duty weekdays, which is when Mundo delivers the mail. So there really wouldn't be an opportunity for anyone else to give him access."

"Did you ever see them have a fight?" Nina asked.

"No."

"Did Mundo ever mention Ray in your . . . um . . . business dealings with him?"

"No."

"Did Ray ever talk about Mundo to you?"

"Nope."

"Howie, how come you got divorced?"

"Huh?"

"I mean, you have two adorable children who you hardly get to see, and now you have to pay women to keep you company."

"Nina, for Godssakes," Jonathan snapped. He turned to Howie. "Forgive her. She has trouble staying on one topic."

"No, it's okay," Howie said. "Look, Nina, I was paying women to keep me company while I was still living with my wife."

It made Nina nervous. Not that Howie and Jonathan were spiritual clones. But it was easier to think that cheating on your wife was something that another generation did. She studied Jonathan's profile. There was so much to worry about. Had he slept with men during art school? Would he sleep with other women during marriage? And that set of worries was entirely independent of her concerns about her own struggles with monogamy and claustrophobia.

"Anyway," Howie continued, "I don't know what more to say about Ray and Mundo. Aside from the fact that Ray clearly knew about Mundo's business, I can't really give you anything more to go on."

"Maybe we should just forget about the whole thing," Jonathan said. "The police aren't hassling me. Let's leave well enough alone."

"Hmm." Nina thought about it for a second, then shook her head. "I guess I don't really believe in the concept of well enough. In the Fischman family, there's no such thing."

CHAPTER 9

"Hey, Nina."

"What?"

"Here's a bone for you to gnaw on." Jonathan handed her a piece of correspondence he had just opened.

She took a look at what he had given her. It was a bill from his cellular phone company for the month of March. "What am I supposed to be gnawing on?"

"Take a look at the phone calls I made."

"What about them? There are hardly any. You haven't even used up your basic monthly charge. Maybe you should discontinue service."

"Nah. Even though I hardly use it, I consider it an insurance policy."

"Against what?"

"Getting stuck in the car. This way I can always call AAA instead of having to tie one of those stupid white handkerchiefs to my antenna."

"Especially since you don't have an antenna." This was something that Nina had learned from hanging around Jonathan. That in some cars, including his, the radio antenna was embedded in the windshield, forcing young thugs to snap off hood ornaments instead. "So what am I looking for?" she asked.

"The outgoing calls."

"What about them?"

"Your sleuthing abilities are apparently on the wane."

Nina went over the statement carefully, but she couldn't come up with anything. "I give up." She handed the bill back to Jonathan.

It was one of those spring evenings that gave you a lot of daylight but not enough warmth to enjoy it by. So that you felt as if you should go for a walk after dinner, but couldn't bring yourself to bundle up and actually get out of the house. Nina had gotten as far as putting on her shoes, but had faltered over finding her gloves and had pretty much abandoned the effort. She flopped into the corner of the couch, making sure to keep her feet off the upholstery. Jonathan's sofa was one of those pale creamy colors favored by people who had neither dogs nor children nor Nina's propensity for putting her shoes all over everything.

"Where was I on March eighteenth?" he asked.

"That's an easy one. It was the day after St. Patrick's Day and we were still in D.C. visiting your friend Lenny. We didn't get back until the nineteenth. Am I right?"

"Right. And where was my phone on the eighteenth?"

"We took the train to Washington and you left the phone in New York. In the car. I remember you bitching about it."

"Right again. So how could I have made a phone call from my mobile phone if I was in Washington and the phone was in my glove compartment in New York?"

"Maybe it's a billing error."

"Maybe. Or . . ."

"Wait a minute. The eighteenth was a Friday. That means that Ray was parking your car. And you don't keep the glove compartment locked, do you?"

"No, I don't."

"So do you think he used your phone?"

"Probably. Or, as you said, it could be a billing error."

"Let's call it and find out." Nina dialed the number. She let it ring at least a dozen times, then hung up.

"Nobody home?" Jonathan asked.

"There's no such thing anymore. There's always a machine home. It's probably a business number. We'll have to try again tomorrow. During office hours."

"I don't know about your machine theory. Maybe Ray was calling home. He didn't seem like the kind of guy who would have an answering machine."

"He couldn't have been calling home," Nina pointed out. "You said he lived in Jackson Heights, didn't you?"

"Yeah."

"Well, that would be a 718 area code. This number is 212, somewhere in Manhattan."

"You're right." Jonathan paused. "I can't figure out why he wouldn't use the pay phone in the lobby."

"Yeah, he was always talking on that phone."

"Maybe he was trying to get through to some bureaucracy about paying some bill or something. Like my insurance company. You always get a busy signal and if you don't have a redial button, you can't get through."

"Does your phone have a redial button?" she asked.

"Yeah, but the lobby pay phone doesn't."

"Or maybe," Nina said, "he needed privacy. He wanted to have a conversation that wouldn't be heard by the porter, or the other tenants, or . . ."

"The mailman?"

"Right."

"I don't know." Jonathan waved his hand dismissively. "It's probably nothing."

"Well, I'm not about to dismiss this so easily. I'm at least going to try this number again tomorrow. Just to see."

By the time Nina got a chance to make the call the next day, it was late afternoon. She had spent the entire day editing draft after draft of motion papers that had to be served before five. It always made her wonder what it would have been like to litigate in the days before word processing. It probably had been more pleasant to mine coal.

Nina's Legal Services office did not compare with the firms she litigated against, with their layers of clerks and paralegals and typists all there to help the lawyers pump out stacks of papers. A process that was environmentally horrifying but effective in impressing the court. Nina felt more like a one-person operation than a cog in a well-oiled machine. She was always fighting the temptation of settling cases in the hallway of the courthouse.

At least she had forced herself, despite her technophobia, to gain a rudimentary command of WordPerfect, which helped turn out drafts. But she had a hard time pushing herself past the basics. It remained beyond her capabilities to paginate and she still had to cut and paste on her hard copy and then cajole someone else into moving everything around on her disk. Pushing the reveal codes keys was still a terrifying experience.

Finally, a little bit past four, she dispatched the messenger with a stack of notices of motion, memoranda of law and affidavits in support thereof. She went back to her desk, kicked the door shut and dialed the number she had copied from Jonathan's mobile phone bill.

A woman answered. "Hello," the voice said warmly. "This is the office of the Public Advocate. Can I help you?"

It was the last thing Nina had expected. She had been prepared for someone speaking Spanish and had mentally rehearsed the opening lines of such a dialogue. But maybe Jonathan had been right. Maybe Ray had been trying to get through to a public agency and had needed a redial button. Except that the woman on the other end of the line did not sound like someone answering calls from the general public. She sounded like she was wearing an expensive suit and either made eighty thousand a year or else was volunteering since money was not important to her.

Nina played a hunch. "Is this his private line?" she asked.

The woman must have been caught off-guard. "Why yes it is," she said, after only a moment of hesitation. She had clearly been bred to be polite. And probably not in the Bronx. "Can I help you?"

"Well, actually I was trying to track down a phone call that was made on my phone to your number. Do you keep a record of incoming calls?"

"Well, I keep a copy of the messages that I take. But if the caller got through to Mr. Carr or didn't leave a message, I would have no record of the call."

She was anything but guarded. Nina figured her for the inner-office secretary, the one who keeps track of social engagements and buys gifts for the Public Advocate's wife. Not the one who does the typing and fields the phone calls from the masses.

"Could you look at your log for March eighteenth of this year and see if there's a call from Ray . . ." Nina searched around for Ray's last name. She finally pictured the *New York Post* article that had featured a snapshot of Ray in a doorman uniform. ". . . Mendez," she said.

The woman was silent for a moment, but nobody is ever really silent. Everyone breathes. And her breathing gave her away. She gave two tiny, almost inaudible gasps and then held her breath. Not the normal breathing pattern of someone sitting comfortably at a desk in a cozy office.

"I'll check," she said tensely. Nina heard the rustle of papers. "No, I don't see anything," the woman said with an obvious sense of relief. Which gave her away again. Her relief was genuine, so her reply must have been truthful . . . She didn't want to lie and was relieved that she didn't have to.

Nina found it comforting to know that there were still some people in the world who were reluctant to lie. Since Nina spent most of her time around lawyers . . . well, not that they really outright lied, but they sort of . . . the thing of it was that lawyers were paid to view the truth as a malleable substance. It was their job to mold it into something that promoted their clients' interests. So you never saw one lawyer yelling at another lawyer "that's not true" because there was a tacit agreement among members of the profession that there wasn't really any such thing as the truth.

This shifting approach to the truth made Nina uncomfortable, but not as uncomfortable as it had when she first entered the profession. There were lawyers who didn't mind at all. The truly great ones, as a matter of fact, all had a slight sociopathic streak. Two parts egomania, two parts narcissism and three parts pathological lying. She tried to picture Roy Cohn, William Kunstler and Alan Dershowitz in fifth grade. She bet that none of them ever raised their hands before they spoke in class.

Anyway, Nina felt for the woman on the other end of the line. She didn't want to force the woman into lying, nor did she want to get her into trouble for revealing too much. But since Nina had gone this far, she felt it imperative to push on.

"Could you check and see if anyone left a message for a call to be returned to 917-555-6030?" It was Jonathan's number—917 was the area code for his mobile phone.

"No, I don't see anything," the woman said in the same relieved tone.

So Ray had either gotten through or had not left a message. And it had to have been Ray. Why else would this woman give two tiny little gasps at the mention of his name? Nina felt as if she had struck pay dirt. The woman was so easy to read. Thank goodness for civilians, because if you had to do all your sleuthing among lawyers, you'd never get anywhere.

CHAPTER 10

Henry Carr was New York City's first Public Advocate.
It was a position that had probably been created by the municipal marketing department, if there was such a thing. It was as if a bunch of local officials had gotten together with their ad agency and asked them to come up with a concept that would be zippy and upbeat. That would make the people of the city feel as though there was someone in their corner. So now there was an 800 number for citizen complaints and the word "watchdog" got tossed around by the press a lot.

But Henry Carr didn't look much like a watchdog. He looked more like an overbred Afghan hound, tall and thin with a long, pointy snout. He was the first WASP since John Lindsay to be elected to a New York citywide office. Like Lindsay, he had a privileged and aristocratic background. That woman who had answered his phone might have been a cousin, or a deb he dated while at Groton. But unlike Lindsay, he lacked an air of confidence. He was broad-shouldered and still had a great crop of hair. But he also had the hangdog expression of a man who knows his time has gone.

WASPs were no longer where it was at in New York City.

Sure, you had to have a healthy supply around, so you could populate the publishing industry and keep the museums open. Besides, you needed some good female specimens to marry off to all those short ethnic financiers that you saw on the society pages, staring lovingly up into the nostrils of their wives. And of course there was still a steady influx of blond gay men from towns all over the country. After all, there weren't enough retired Jewish schoolteachers to sell out a season at the Met. But a heterosexual male WASP actually getting enough votes to be elected to office?

Nina fully expected to be wandering around the Museum of Natural History someday and stumble across a little exhibit right next to the Hall of Dinosaurs. "The WASP Politician" the plaque would read. And there would be a six-foot-two skeleton with a swimmer's build. And the sign would explain that the species was extinct.

Nina remembered how Henry Carr had gotten himself elected Public Advocate. Although she hated to read about international and national politics, the way she hated to see movies in which men drove motorcycles through plate-glass windows, she remained a great fan of the *Metro Section* of the *Times*. She recalled that Henry Carr had been pitted against two tough opponents in the Democratic Primary, an Italian and a Jew. The Jew was a woman, the Italian a man. The Italian guy had been leading the pack throughout much of the race. If the day of the male WASP was over, the male Italian was just hitting his stride. Mario, Rudy, Alphonse, even Regis Philbin had an Italian mother. It made you think that the next skeleton in the museum to be marked extinct might be that of a Jewish politician, five foot six with an accountant's build.

So the Italian guy was way ahead, with Carr and the Jewish woman limping along behind him, when scandal hit. It turned out that the front-runner had a brother who had been named one of New York City's ten worst landlords by *The Village Voice* for seven years running. And Carr's other opponent had a no-show sister-in-law on her Board of Education payroll. Carr came from behind to win the primary and later the election. And there he remained, the token WASP in City Hall.

All this ran through Nina's mind in the ten seconds after her call to Carr's secretary ended. She called Jonathan and described the conversation. "So what the hell was Ray doing calling Henry Carr's private number?" she asked him.

"Maybe they went to high school together."

"Hah. Good one." She hunched up one shoulder so that she could hold the phone and still have both hands free to collate. It was a bad telephone habit that she couldn't break, along with wearing post earrings that stabbed you behind your left ear whenever you held the receiver to your head.

"What are you doing?" he asked. "I hear rustling."

"Collating. I forgot to push the sort button on the Xerox machine."

"Why didn't you just stop the machine and reset it?"

"I hate to push stop in the middle of a job. The same way I hate returning clothes. It's just not worth the trouble."

"I see." He was either being mocking or indulgent, she couldn't tell which. "You haven't finished your court papers yet? It's almost five. How are you going to get them served today?"

"Oh, I sent those out a while ago. I'm on to the next case already." Nina wondered if there was a world where people actually did one thing at a time. And drank coffee in between, like in the movies.

"Maybe Ray was working for Henry Carr," Jonathan said.

"Doing what? Moving his car from side to side of the street?"

"Maybe."

"Oh, please. I'm sure that the Carrs do not have the kind of money they used to. That their fortunes have dwindled since the nineteenth century, when they sold off their half of the lower Hudson River Valley for what proved to be a ridiculously low price. But even though the sun has set on the Carr empire, I'm sure Henry can still afford to garage his car."

"Well, maybe Ray was doing something else for him."

"Like feeding his cat?" she said. "Somehow I don't see it. I'm sure he has household help. I hear that his wife is loaded."

"How do you know that?"

"I know someone who works in his office. Charlotte Klein. She used to work for Legal Services. According to Charlotte, he has one of those Texan wives who comes from an oil family. One that managed to hold on to their money. She's very flashy, big diamonds, big hair, big trust fund."

"So Charlotte Klein knows all about her boss's personal finances?"

"Of course," Nina said. "What do you think lawyers gossip about? Their cases?"

"No, I'm sure they don't."

"Anyway, according to Charlotte, Mrs. Carr is very society conscious. You know how those new-money Texas types are. Always trying to prove that they're not inferior to the old guard, like her husband. I'll bet his wife's got a whopper of a mother-in-law problem."

"I didn't realize that you were such an expert on new and old money."

"I'm a people person," Nina said. "Actually, I'm partial to all mammals."

"I see. Anyway, Henry Carr's wife . . . what's her name?"

"I don't remember."

"So Mrs. Carr is loaded. And you don't think that Henry had to hire Ray to move his car or feed his cat. That he parks his car in a garage and has live-in help. Where does he live?"

"I don't know," she said. "Where do people like that live? Probably in your neighborhood. But over on Park or Fifth."

"So why do you think that Ray made that call?"

"Maybe he was working for Carr. But not feeding his cat. Doing something illegal."

"Nina, your imagination is becoming hyperactive. Does Henry Carr strike you as the kind of guy who's involved in illegal activities? I mean, he seems like the antithesis of a mob-connected politician."

"Don't automatically fall for that preppy wholesomeness. You know, the Mafia makes sure that their sons get Ivy League educations. Carr could have roomed with a second-generation don."

"So you're an expert on that too now?"

"Not an expert."

"Well, what do you base your information on?"

"Ummm . . . Al Pacino in *The Godfather*. Didn't he go to Princeton or Dartmouth or somewhere?"

"Nina, you're a bullshit artist, that's what you are."

"It's not my fault. Bullshitting is what they happen to teach in law school these days."

"So you think that Henry Carr's prep school roommate is a son of the Mafia? I don't know."

"But Ray must have been on Carr's payroll in some capacity. What other connection could there be between these two men?"

"Why don't you call Henry Carr and ask him?" Jonathan said.

"Or better yet, I'll ask him in person."

"How are you going to do that?"

"I have my ways."

"Right. Henry Carr is going to meet with you just because you're curious."

"Wanna bet?" Nina asked.

"Yeah."

"How much?"

"I'll bet you our summer vacation," Jonathan said.

"What do you mean?"

"If you win, you get to decide where we go. If I win, I decide."

"Oh." Nina hadn't really thought about their summer vacation. She hadn't let herself. Because she wasn't sure there was going to be one. Well, she thought, there probably would be, since if they were talking about moving in together, then it should be understood that they were taking their vacation together. But assumptions were dangerous. She had learned that lesson well. So she was moved by Jonathan's attitude about it, that it wasn't even a question. She pushed her stack of collated papers to the rear of her desk and leaned back in her chair.

"Well, is it a deal?" he asked.

"That depends."

"On what?"

"On what I have to lose. You're not thinking of going to golf camp, are you?"

"Golf camp? Hey, I hadn't thought of it, but now that you mention it, it sounds great."

"Me and my mouth."

"Yeah, you and your mouth. What a pair."

"All right, it's a deal," she said. "How long do I get to set up a meeting with Carr?"

"How long do you need?"

She gave the standard answer for court adjournments. "I need three weeks, Your Honor."

"Granted," he said.

Nina was already fumbling through her Rolodex by the time Jonathan hung up the phone.

CHAPTER 11

Charlotte Klein answered her own phone. She had the perfect public service phone voice. As she spoke the words "Charlotte Klein," she managed to convey a guarded yet competent air. She was glad to hear from Nina, or at least professed to be.

"It's been quite a while," Charlotte said. "What have you been up to?"

"Nothing dramatic. Still stuck in this office. I think I'm starting to mold."

"Well, as I've told you before, you should consider coming here."

"I know. But I always had this fantasy that when I leave this job with its crummy salary, I'd go to one without a crummy salary."

"Like what?"

"I don't know. Maybe someone will give me a talk show. On radio, so I wouldn't have to watch my weight."

"Dream on. Let's face it, Nina, you're the crummy salary type. Born for the public sector."

"I guess. Besides, if you go work for a firm, you always have to be bringing your shoes in to be repaired."

"And your brows waxed."

"Right." The era of the unplucked brow appeared to be over and Nina mourned its passing. She had enjoyed it while it lasted, but now grappled with the issue of whether or not to take action. So far she had remained paralyzed and continued to sport a look somewhere between Brooke Shields and John L. Lewis. "Seriously," she said, "is the Public Advocate really looking for another staff attorney?"

"He's always on the lookout for someone who's intelligent and willing to be underpaid. Are you interested?"

She knew she was manipulating Charlotte, but it seemed like the prudent approach. Nina wasn't sure how close a relationship her friend had with her boss. If Nina revealed her true agenda, Charlotte might feel compelled to protect Carr. Or if she went ahead and conspired, setting up a meeting so that Nina could grill him, and Carr found out, he'd blame Charlotte. As long as Nina kept her motives to herself, Charlotte could maintain her innocence.

"I would be interested," Nina said. "Could you get me an interview?"

"Sure."

"Uh, how many layers would I have to go through before I got to meet with Carr?"

"We're not that big an agency. Usually Henry has Ed Kornbluth, his chief aide, interview candidates. If Eddie likes you, you get straight to Henry."

"His aide, huh?" Nina was going for a disappointed tone without sounding bratty.

Charlotte fell for it. "Would you rather see Henry first?"

"That would be great."

"Just fax me your résumé and I'll see what I can do."

"Yeah, my résumé." It was a sore point with Nina. Every now and then, someone would say "Fax me your résumé." It was like telling her to pull down her pants. Because her résumé revealed something even worse than her thighs. There was no way to disguise the fact that after graduating from law school, she had started doing something she didn't like doing very much. And that she had spent thirteen years doing it over and over again. Without even getting promoted.

Not that she had been passed over for promotions that she had sought. Becoming management in a Legal Services office was a traumatic step. It was a break from everything you had become familiar and comfortable with. It meant leaving the union, which was something akin to converting to Catholicism. And then you had to manage people. Which might seem like a normal thing to do to some people. But for the red diaper babies, the children of the left, it was a step that required multiple therapy sessions. Ida and Leo Fischman had not raised their daughter to write up employee tardiness or draft memos regarding dress codes.

But if Nina's lack of promotions was explainable, it was more difficult to explain why she had never gotten herself another job. The truth was that it was hard to leave the nest. Any nest, she supposed. Even a nest made out of thorny twigs. Her office was like a dysfunctional family. You wanted to leave home, but you couldn't be sure that you could function on the outside. Even though you weren't really functioning on the inside.

From time to time, she would get out her résumé and try to be creative. She'd redraft her job description over and over, but her efforts were pointless. It was as if someone had stamped the page with big letters: T-R-A-P-P-E-D.

"Yeah, my résumé," Nina repeated.

"Do you have a current one?" Charlotte asked.

"The one I have has been current for thirteen years. As I said, there's mold growing on me."

"Try to think of your long-term commitment to Legal Services as evidencing single-mindedness, loyalty and a sense of purpose."

"You sound like a public relations person instead of a lawyer."

"What do you think we do here?"

"I guess I don't really know," Nina said.

"You've never worked for a politician, have you?"

"No."

"Well, when you work for an elected official, what you do all day is try to get his name into the paper."

"I could do that. I could do anything if it meant that I didn't have to go to Housing Court."

She didn't really mean it. Things weren't *that* bad. Not as bad as the summer she drove a cab in New York back in college. The cab wasn't air-conditioned and she drove during the day, when the city was at its hottest and traffic at its worst. Nina remembered sitting behind the wheel and envying anyone who was a pedestrian. Walking seemed like the most glamorous activity imaginable at the time.

It wasn't *that* bad, but almost. Nina would sit in Housing Court on a weekday morning and envy anyone who wasn't there. The commercial trial part across the hall seemed glamorous, as if the people in there were sipping champagne cocktails and humming Cole Porter tunes.

Maybe the way things were playing out was fortuitous. Maybe she would never get to the bottom of why Ray Mendez had called Henry Carr, or who was responsible for Ray's murder. But maybe she'd get a new job. Maybe she'd be able to get on the subway and head downtown every morning without feeling as if she were walking to the electric chair. She'd take the express to Chambers Street and walk east into the sun to the Municipal Building. She'd get to the office, grab a cup of coffee from the communal pot, glance at the *Times,* make some calls and then attend a meeting. All on a carpeted floor.

It was a nice fantasy. Of course, it was possible that the Public Advocate's office was a bigger dump than hers. Maybe they had metal folding chairs too. But somehow she doubted it. The woman who'd answered her call to Henry Carr's private line definitely sounded as if her butt spent the day on upholstery.

"Listen, Charlotte, I don't know if I'm what your office is looking for. And I don't know if I'm really ready to make a change. After all, it's only been thirteen years, I wouldn't want to do anything premature. But I would like to at least interview with Carr."

"Okay. As soon as I get your résumé, I'll trot it over to him."

"I'm already on my way to the fax machine. What's your number?"

Once Nina had scribbled down Charlotte's number, she turned her attention to her résumé. It needed something, that was for sure. But it wasn't like a pot of soup that you could just add seasoning to. She couldn't very well stick white water rafting into her Hobbies and Interests section just because it looked good. Not when she'd never been on a raft in her life. Oh well, she'd have to do what Charlotte had suggested. Play up her sense of commitment and loyalty to a job that she was obviously desperate to leave.

CHAPTER 12

Henry Carr's handshake was a little watery, like his
blue eyes. He dripped instead of squeezed. His appearance
didn't exactly summon up the word "advocate."

He didn't seem very "public" either, with his private
school look. He was strictly superannuated preppy—tousled
hair parted on the side, sort of hanging over one eye, a blue
buttoned-down shirt with the sleeves rolled up and beat-up
penny loafers. All that was missing was a lacrosse stick.

"Please sit down." He gestured toward a club chair that
was, as Nina expected, well upholstered. The room had a
comfortable feeling, tinged with a touch of shabbiness. Like
Henry Carr's shoes. The perfect setting for a prep school boy
in the public sector. The chair Nina sat in was covered with a
dark green fabric, the color Nina always associated with
men's clubs. The association was not made from firsthand
experience, of course. There was a lot of well-worn brown
leather around the room, not just on Henry Carr's feet. His
briefcase, his book bindings, even his desk blotter seemed
just the tiniest bit scuffed.

There was a credenza under the window that held photos
of a younger Henry Carr (same haircut) with Robert Ken-

nedy, as well as a shot of Carr shaking hands with Mario Cuomo and Bill Clinton. The credenza also supported an eight-by-ten family portrait (framed in worn green leather) of Carr with his wife and two teenage children. The kids were darker versions of Carr, with the brown eyes and hair of their mother.

Mrs. Carr had the kind of Texas beauty that Nina had never understood. That broad, flat face that, back in the days when Miss America used to be white and Southern, always popped up in beauty pageants. It wasn't a look Nina considered beautiful; it reminded her of Lyndon Johnson's daughters. The kind of faces you picture surrounded by a brunette flip and a twirling baton.

Mrs. Carr had that same look with dark eyes, probably a touch of a Cherokee legacy. But her brown hair was far from a flip. It was quite Madison Avenue, tousled like her husband's, but in a deliberate way. And lots of it. She could have been a magazine illustration for an article entitled "Luxuriant Tresses." The clothes were cut stylishly, but too brightly colored for a New York native.

And no Manhattan resident would accessorize a red suit with navy. Mrs. Carr's necklace featured pavé diamonds, the jewelry equivalent of navy and red. In the center of the pavé, however, nestled a real rock, multiple carats, that made a statement. What the statement was probably depended on the observer. To Nina it said "I don't have to ride the subway."

"Thank you for seeing me," Nina said as she shook Henry Carr's hand.

"You're welcome," he said politely. It was a phrase that Nina always forgot to use. Never saying "You're welcome" was a New York affliction. New Yorkers just never bothered. It wasn't that they were rude, or that the other person wasn't welcome. "You're welcome" just wasn't part of the city's lexicon.

Nina never thought twice about it, except when she was giving directions to out-of-towners in the street. She'd point the way, and they'd say "Thank you" and Nina would be off. And sometimes she'd notice that they'd still be standing there expectantly so she'd yell over her shoulder "You're welcome" and then they'd look satisfied.

But Henry Carr used the phrase with great ease and did make her feel welcome. His blue eyes might be watery and have a defeated look to them, but at least he managed to maintain eye contact. Which was more than a lot of guys Nina had faced on the other side of the desk could do.

"So you used to work with Charlotte, is that right?" he asked.

Nina could tell that she was going to have to take hold of the conversational reins. There was nothing on her résumé for a guy like Carr to grab on to. No fancy schools, no Waspy law firms, no Episcopalian church choirs. And getting the conversation around to Ray's murder was not going to be an easy task. She should have plotted this out better.

"Yes, I work in a federally funded Legal Services office that services the elderly indigent. Charlotte was a colleague of mine until you stole her away from us."

"She really knows how to deal with the elderly public. I guess she learned that working in your office."

"Well, she was lucky to leave when she did. Things have really gotten worse in this city recently. For everyone, but especially for the elderly."

"Indeed." He was getting the glazed look that all politicians get when people start complaining to them. Nina knew that she had better steer the conversation straight to Ray before she lost him permanently.

"Even the ones who live in decent neighborhoods. For

example, we service a large population on the Upper East Side. You'd think they'd feel relatively secure."

"Mmm." He was getting truly bored.

"But I bet that you don't even feel secure on the Upper East Side these days."

"I don't know. I'm not there very much."

"Oh." Nina got stopped short. Her conversational plans were going awry. "Where do you live?"

"Brooklyn Heights."

"Really? Did you grow up there?"

"As a matter of fact I did."

"How interesting," she said.

"Why is it interesting?" He seemed amused rather than annoyed. Which earned him points, since a lot of men found questions like that intrusive. That was unfortunate for Nina, since those were the only kinds of questions that had answers she was interested in. She was already imagining Henry Carr as a young chap in the fifties, attending St. Ann's Church on Sunday and wearing the uniform of the Packer Collegiate Institute.

"I find it interesting that you grew up in Brooklyn Heights because . . . um . . . I don't know, that's just the kind of person I am. I like to know things like that."

He smiled and leaned back in his chair. "When I was growing up, Brooklyn Heights was like a small town." He looked dreamily out the window.

So Henry Carr was the kind of guy who'd rather look out the window than go on and on about the duties of the Public Advocate. Maybe Nina really should consider working here.

"A small town, huh?" she said. "Well, I can't say the same for the Bronx of my childhood. But at least you used to be able to take a walk after dinner without wearing a bullet-proof vest."

"I miss those days. I really do." Henry Carr gave her a sad

look. No, wait a minute, it was more than sad. It was tortured. Something was really eating this guy.

"I miss those days too," Nina said. It was ridiculous, of course, to pretend that they were missing the same days. First of all, the guy had about ten years on her. So when he was listening to "Captain Marvel" on the radio, Nina wasn't even around yet. And as far as idyllic childhood memories went, by the time Nina got to junior high school, kids were already running around with hypodermic syringes. Besides, Nina was sure that the women on Henry Carr's block wore coatdresses instead of housedresses. Coatdresses with pillbox hats and alligator purses. But New York was the kind of city where people tried to pretend that class distinctions didn't matter. That this was a city of strivers and hustlers and it didn't matter where you came from.

Which was a crock. Well, maybe places like Philadelphia were worse. Nina didn't know and she didn't want to find out.

"Those days are gone forever," Carr said, again looking tortured. Yeah, if she were him, she'd miss those days too. The days when all some rich white guy had to do was show up for life and he had it made.

"It's the guns that are the most troublesome," Nina said, trying to get the conversation around to Ray's murder. "If we could only control the firearms, the city would be livable. I have a friend who lives in a very nice building in the East Eighties. And you know what just happened there?"

"What?"

"His doorman was shot."

"Really." Nina scrutinized Henry Carr's face for his reaction. But since he had looked so tortured to begin with, it was hard to tell. She thought he looked even more tortured now, but she couldn't be sure.

"Did you read about it?" she asked.

"Um, maybe."

"The doorman was in a car at the time. Parked in front of the building. And no one has any idea why it happened. It seems like just one of those senseless random acts of violence."

Henry Carr was whitening visibly as she went on. He definitely looked nervous. "So tell me, Ms. Fischman, what interested you in applying to the Public Advocate's office?" He bit at a cuticle.

She considered telling him to call her Nina. But then he might feel compelled to tell her to call him Henry and then he'd resent it. So she let the "Ms. Fischman" go. "Well," she said, "Charlotte got me interested initially." Damn, he had veered the conversation away from Ray and now she had no idea how to get it back.

"Yes, so what do you know about us?" He was really working hard on that cuticle. No more dreamily looking out the window. Actually, he looked like he was about to plotz.

"What appeals to me about the job," she recited from rote, as Charlotte had coached, "is the opportunity to serve the public in a broader way. At Legal Services we work mostly on a case-by-case basis, serving the individual. We've been accused of taking a Band-Aid approach. With some justification, I'm afraid. I'd like to be able to do something for a wider group of people for a change."

"Haven't you been involved in any class action litigation in all the years you've been there?"

She winced a little at "all the years." "Of course I have," she said. "And class action suits can be exciting. But they're also problematic in their own way. What with getting bogged down in discovery motions and all."

"I see." He looked a little put off.

Shit, Nina told herself. Now she sounded like a kvetch. She didn't like little cases and she didn't like big ones. She'd better find something to be enthusiastic about. "Actually, I have been involved in some interesting impact litigation using various elderly groups as the plaintiffs. And I think that, as a result, I have something to offer an office such as yours." Charlotte had told her to play up her experience with the elderly, since Carr's weakest vote-getting was in the neighborhoods with the oldest populations.

"Yes?" He did look interested. Although still nervously working on that cuticle.

"During the past years, I've gotten to know various staff members of almost every major agency that services the elderly in the city. And I think we could do very effective outreach, getting you out there, making sure they recognize you and know that you're working for them."

"That sounds very good."

"And although my office is located in Manhattan, I've worked with elderly groups all over the boroughs. I can guarantee you exposure from Brighton Beach to Riverdale to South Ozone Park. Especially in the Bronx, my home turf." Charlotte had told her to hammer away at the borough angle since Carr, in addition to a poor showing among the elderly, had trouble in the city's outlying neighborhoods. She told Nina it was hell getting him to take a trip out to anyplace that had two-family houses. He'd rather walk around Harlem at three in the morning, Charlotte had said, than shake hands with anyone who bowled.

"Excellent." Carr nodded enthusiastically.

"And as a result of my work in the community, I've also developed a network of press contacts. And a clear idea of what kind of stories they're looking for." It was basically bullshit. But she did have a very brief affair years ago with a science reporter for the *New York Times*. And a woman she had attended college with had a regular segment on National Public Radio's "Weekend Edition."

101

"Listen, I'd like you to meet Eddie. But he won't be in until later in the week." Charlotte had also explained that Carr would never hire anyone without consulting Ed Kornbluth. Eddie was more than just Carr's right nut, Charlotte had said. He was his guide dog as Carr stumbled around in a city of people he had nothing in common with.

"I'd love to meet Eddie." She knew enough not to ask Henry Carr any questions about the job. Just plant the idea that you can get his name in the paper and get out of there.

"I'll introduce you to Prudence on your way out. She should be back from lunch by now. She'll set something up."

She would bet anything that Prudence was the woman who had answered Henry Carr's private line the first time Nina called. She had talked to her again when Nina called to set up the interview. On her way in, Nina had noticed an empty desk with a Tiffany perpetual desk calendar on it. It had to be Prudence.

Carr led Nina out to the reception area. "Pru, set something up with Eddie for Ms. Fischman, won't you?" he said to the Jackie Onassis clone seated behind the desk.

"Certainly." The voice matched perfectly.

"Nice meeting you." Henry Carr shook Nina's hand. "Thanks for coming by."

"You're welcome," Nina remembered to say.

After he retreated to his office, Prudence turned to Nina. "Actually," she said, "Mr. Kornbluth has asked me not to make any more appointments without checking with him first. So could I give you a call when he gets back to town?"

"Of course." Nina told her where she could be reached.

As she waited in the hallway of the Municipal Building for the elevator, Nina found herself working on a cuticle of her own. What was she going to do now? Carr had visibly blanched at the mention of Ray's name, but she was no closer to understanding the connection between the two of them than she had been when she came up in the elevator. Meanwhile, she had set herself up for a second interview. For a job as what seemed, for all intents and purposes, to be that of a press agent. Was that what she had gone to law school for?

What had she gone to law school for anyway? Who remembered? Oh well, she told herself as the elevator door opened, at least she'd gotten a meeting with Carr and won the bet with Jonathan. Which meant that she wouldn't have to go to golf camp.

CHAPTER 13

"So what does this guy look like?" Jonathan asked.

"Don't you remember? When he was running for office he gave a bunch of press conferences. He was all over the media," Nina said.

"Who pays attention to what the New York City Public Advocate looks like? What the hell does he do, anyway?"

"As far as I can tell, all he does is get elected. Wait a minute." She rummaged through her purse. "Here." She pulled out a booklet. "It's his annual report. I picked it up while I was waiting outside his office. I'm sure it has a photograph of him somewhere in it."

"I'm sure it does." Jonathan sounded snide.

"Yeah, well, that's the stuff that gets politicians out of bed in the morning. Their day is just one big photo-op." Nina thumbed through Henry Carr's annual report. "Lots of photos of the man. Here's a good one." She handed it to Jonathan, who was seated at his dining room table paying bills.

He pushed his checkbook over to one side and placed the annual report in front of him. It was a picture of Henry Carr taken with a bunch of Dominicans up in Washington

Heights. He looked like a giraffe that got caught in the penguin pavilion. "A real man of the people," Jonathan said.

"Yeah, right."

"He looks familiar."

"Well, as I said, he had a bunch of press conferences—"

"No." Jonathan interrupted her. "I don't mean that. I think I've seen him in the building."

"Really?"

"I think so."

"He lives in Brooklyn Heights," Nina said. "Besides, a guy like Carr would really stand out in a postwar building like this. He's so . . . I don't know . . . prewar, I guess."

"I know what you mean. Guys like him don't usually go east of Lexington. Unless they're on Sutton Place."

"You're starting to sound like me. It's scary."

"I know."

"Anyway," Nina said, "if you did see him in the building, you might be very likely to remember him. Because of the incongruity."

"Yeah, but I could be imagining it. Maybe I just saw him on the subway or something. But you know what we should do?"

"What?"

"Ask Howie. He spends more time in the building than I do. Let's ask him if he's ever seen Carr in the lobby or the elevator."

"Or the laundry room," Nina added.

"Um, I don't think it was the laundry room."

"No, he's definitely not a laundry room kind of guy. I wonder if he knows such things exist."

"I'm going to give Howie a call." Jonathan went into the kitchen and got his cordless phone. He brought it into the living room where Nina sprawled on the couch. "The Manhattan directory is over there in the bookcase. If you look up his number, I'll call him."

Nina considered voicing her objection to doing the scut work, but Jonathan seemed to be on a detecting roll and she didn't want to stem the tide. "I don't even know his last name," she said, whining just a bit to half-drive the point home.

"Mandel."

"Oh, right. How could I forget?" She looked up his number. Jonathan had been right. He wasn't the only Howie Mandel. There were half a dozen other Howard Mandels, and that was in Manhattan alone. "Here it is." Were they making the print smaller in these things or was she getting old? Did they make large print editions of the phone book or were the visually handicapped compelled to use directory assistance all the time? And if there were large print editions, how much did they weigh? Whatever. She gave Jonathan the phone number and he dialed it.

"Hey, Howie, it's Jonathan. How's it going? . . . Oh yeah? So do you want to call me back after you take a shower? . . . Oh, okay . . . Listen, Nina and I are still trying to figure out who killed Ray. And why. We sort of stumbled on something that could be a clue. I want to show you a picture of this guy I think I've seen in the building. And I want you to tell me whether he looks familiar to you. Whether you've seen him hanging around in the lobby or something . . . Okay, sure, we'll be here." Jonathan hung up.

"So?" Nina said.

"He'll be over as soon as he gets out of the shower. He just got back from playing tennis."

"Big surprise. Doesn't anybody in this building work, for Chrissakes?"

"Don't yell. Besides, it's almost seven. He could have been working all day and played a quick set afterward."

"Yeah, right. So if it is Henry Carr that you've seen in the building, I wonder what he was doing here. Since he lives in Brooklyn."

"Who knows?"

"Maybe he has a regular tennis partner who lives here," Nina said. "And they meet downstairs before their game. After all, playing tennis is all anyone in this building seems to do. But wait a minute."

"What?"

"Carr told me during our interview that he didn't spend much time in this neighborhood. So are you saying that you've seen him around on a regular basis?"

"Well, I don't know about regular," Jonathan said. "But I think I've seen him here from time to time."

"Then he lied. And he looked extremely nervous. Interesting, no?"

Jonathan nodded as the doorbell rang. "Well, that was fast," he said as he opened the door. Howie came in, wearing an NYU sweatshirt.

"I decided to take a shower later. I hope you don't mind."

"Of course not."

"Now, what's going on?" Howie asked.

"Take a look at this photo." Jonathan handed him the annual report. "I think I've seen this guy in the building. Am I imagining it, or have you seen him too?"

Howie didn't hesitate at all. "Sure, I've seen him. A couple of times. In the mailroom, talking to Mundo."

"Are you sure?"

"Absolutely. A guy like this you remember."

"How come?"

"He doesn't look real. He looks like the kind of guy they put in the movies to play a role. Not that he's so good-looking. I don't mean that he looks like a movie star or anything. But he doesn't look like a regular guy who's just getting his mail."

"Howie," Nina said tartly, "haven't you ever seen a WASP before? Outside of the movies, I mean."

"Nina, you said yourself a minute ago that a guy like Carr would stand out in this building. Why are you giving Howie a hard time?" Jonathan said.

"I've seen plenty of WASPs," Howie said. "I went to college in Syracuse. The whole city was blond. Except for the Italians. But nobody looked like this."

"He's a rich one," Nina said. "They're different."

Howie turned to the cover of the annual report. "So is he the Public Advocate? Is that the story?"

"That's the story. His name is Henry Carr."

"Huh. So the Public Advocate of the City of New York is a client of Mundo's. Whaddya know."

"Are you sure he's a client?"

"Oh, yeah. I could tell by the way they were talking. This guy was definitely availing himself of Mundo's services. So do you think this has something to do with Ray's murder?"

"I got this phone bill this month," Jonathan said. "And we think that Ray made a phone call to Henry Carr on my car phone. And we're trying to figure out why."

"Well, it's gotta be blackmail," Howie said. "Ray knew that this Carr guy was frequenting hookers and he was blackmailing him."

Nina and Jonathan nodded at each other. "Yeah, I think that Howie's right," Nina said. "Carr couldn't have gotten into the building to talk to Mundo without Ray's cooperation. So Ray must have known what was going on."

"Well . . ." Jonathan said, sounding doubtful.

"Look, Carr didn't live in this building, right?" Nina said.

"Right."

"So how did he get into the mailroom?" she asked. "He must have said something to Ray to gain access. So maybe he told him that he wanted to see Mundo and Ray figured out who Carr was. And then he decided that it would be a good opportunity to put the squeeze on him. Make some extra cash, more than he could make parking cars or feeding cats."

"Look, it's a theory," Jonathan said. "But it could be totally wrong."

"It sounds right to me," Howie said. "I mean, it makes so much sense. You know what you guys should do?"

"What?"

"Ask Mundo."

"I don't know," Jonathan said. "Last time I tried to talk to him, he laughed in my face. I doubt whether all of a sudden he'd decide to reveal the contents of his client list."

"You want me to talk to him? Or better yet, come with me. I'm a client. If I'm there, he'll at least talk to you."

"I'm only second in command here." Jonathan looked toward Nina.

"All right, I'll go with you, Howie," she said. "Just tell me when is convenient for you."

"Tomorrow's fine."

"Okay."

"Nina, you said you had a ton of work to do. That you couldn't even have lunch with some friend who was in from out of town because you had to get out some papers."

"Well, I didn't really want to see her anyway. And I'll get the papers done, even if I have to work this weekend."

"Boy," Jonathan said, "you're really getting obsessed with this."

"Just wait," Nina said. "By the time this is over, you'll be sorry you ever moved into a doorman building."

CHAPTER 14

Howie rang Jonathan's bell at eleven-thirty the next morning. Nina had been having a pleasurable morning, pretending she was in a hotel. Being alone in someone else's house was a treat. No panty hose to wash, no mail to sort through, no plants to water. It wasn't a situation that occurred often. Not like when she was a teenager, when she used to baby-sit and the kids would go to sleep. Then she'd have the same feeling. She'd take a tour of the kitchen cabinets as if she were in an art museum, and then settle into an armchair and read *TV Guide*. It was like flying. You got to read periodicals that normally you weren't dumb enough to bother with.

Jonathan didn't have any moronic reading material, but she did turn on the "Joan Rivers Show." Which wasn't really the electronic equivalent. It was trashy, but not dumb. It always amazed Nina how irreverent people like Joan Rivers could hang around rich Republicans. Didn't they just make her barf?

Joan Rivers was interviewing Cindy Adams when Nina turned her off. She just couldn't handle that many facelifts at once. Between the two of them they must have been responsible for their plastic surgeon's entire Southampton renovation. Nina pulled a hardcover biography of Laurence Olivier from Jonathan's bookcase. She went straight for the chapter about Olivier's affair with Danny Kaye. The *New York Times* review of the book had mentioned it, and she had always meant to find out more. Nina hadn't quite finished the chapter when Howie arrived.

"See this guy?" She showed Howie the photo on the cover.

"Yeah?"

"It's Sir Laurence Olivier. Did you know that he and Danny Kaye were lovers?"

"Really?" Howie didn't look like he could get into it, so Nina put the book back on the shelf. When she'd first heard about it, she'd had a lot more to say than "really." She had thought about it for days. Such an odd couple. The fact that they were both men was the least of it.

"Ready?" she said.

"Yup."

"I really appreciate this."

"No problem." Howie shrugged. "I'm sort of getting into it."

Suddenly Nina felt attracted to him. She shooed the emotion away, since there was no point to it. He wasn't her type. Oh, he seemed decent and he was certainly being helpful. And he was good-looking enough. But she knew to stay away. It wasn't just that he was Jonathan's friend. Or that he ran around with prostitutes. Or that he seemed like the kind of guy who would wear a toupee if he lost his hair. Or that he wasn't all that interested in the Olivier-Kaye love affair.

The thing that was wrong with Howie was that he was a regular guy. And regular guys were the most dangerous. Because they were so unobtainable. A guy like Howie, with his sneakers and jeans and season tickets to the Mets, threw Nina right back to her adolescence. When even though she had told herself that the boys in sneakers lacked a unique world vision, she would have given anything for one of them to think she was cute. And all the years spent in trying to get over that—in expanding her horizons and traveling everywhere; in hanging out with multicultural people with various sexual preferences; in dating men who rooted for the Red Sox and other tortured teams—none of it helped.

Because it all faded away when she came upon a Mets fan, a regular guy. And she would ache for him to think she was cute. It was probably why Jerry Seinfeld popped up in her dreams so often. Of course, she could tell herself that her fascination with Seinfeld was really an obsession with Larry David, who wrote most of the scripts and was the brain behind the face. And who was bald and wore glasses and was older and more tortured than Jerry. And who was a Yankee fan. But that was denial.

Jonathan rooted for the Chicago Cubs, the most neurotic team of all.

She thought about all this as she locked the door and rode down in the elevator with Howie. She could tell by the way he was standing that he was uncomfortable. That it wouldn't have occurred to him to take a woman with him to go have a chat with a pimp about a john. And that he was probably sorry that he had volunteered to talk to Mundo. And Nina was sure he didn't think she was cute. The excursion began taking on "let's get this over with" instead of "isn't this fun" overtones.

Mundo was already in the mailroom when they got there. He gave Howie half of a wave and looked at Nina without enthusiasm.

"How ya' doin'?" Howie asked him.

Mundo just nodded and waited.

"This is a friend of mine," Howie said. "Nina Fischman."
Mundo nodded again.

"We wanted to ask you something."

"Okay."

"We wanted to ask you if you know a guy named Henry Carr."

Nina watched closely for Mundo's reaction. But he reacted no more strongly than when Howie had introduced her. The name Henry Carr did not summon up any more emotion than did the name Nina Fischman. Mundo just gave them his by now familiar nod.

"Is that a yes?" It came out before Nina could stop herself.

Howie shot her a look. A look with a deep and evident history. A look that he had used for his mother, possibly an older sister and, she was sure, his ex-wife. A look that spoke of an epic struggle with all the Jewish women in his life.

"Uh, Mundo," Howie said, rubbing his nose as if to convey casualness, "so you know this guy?"

"I know Mr. Carr." Mundo took out his master key, turned around and unlocked a row of mailboxes.

"Yeah, I thought so." Howie moved over, back into Mundo's line of vision. "I thought I saw him talking to you down here."

"I know that his name's Henry Carr because somebody told me. But he calls himself something else. I guess he didn't want me to know his real name."

"Well, you know why, don't you?" Nina asked.

"He's a big deal down at City Hall," Howie said. Nina considered explaining that Carr's office was actually in the Municipal Building, but she didn't want to get that look again.

"Yeah, I know," Mundo said.

"So you fix him up sometimes?" Howie asked, pointing his nose in a general upstairs direction.

"No more." Mundo shook his head with more animation that he had previously displayed.

"Why not?"

"He's a pain." Mundo picked a bundle of mail out of a bag lying on the floor. He began putting the mail into the appropriate boxes. "Too much trouble," he said.

"What kind of trouble?" Howie asked.

"He bothers one of my girls."

"Really? Henry Carr?" Nina asked. "He doesn't look like the kind of guy who would bother anybody."

This time Howie gave her a little nudge with his elbow instead of a look. "What did he do? Rough her up?"

"No. He just follows her around. Watches her. Calls her. Makes her nervous."

Nina couldn't picture Henry Carr stalking. But she kept her mouth shut.

"Who's he bothering?" Howie asked. "Somebody upstairs?"

"Kristen. You know her?"

"The one with the cats on the twenty-sixth floor?"

"That's her."

"She's a great-looking broad. I could see how somebody could get hung up on her."

"She's gonna be around this weekend, if you're interested," Mundo said. He said it casually, as if he were reciting a movie schedule.

"My kids are going to be in this weekend. I think they're a little young for Kristen. We're gonna stick to the Knicks."

"Suit yourself."

"Nina, is there anything specific you wanted to ask Mundo?" Howie didn't look as though he meant it.

"One thing," Nina said, despite Howie's look of impatience. "Did you ever see Carr talking to Ray the doorman?"

"I don't know." Mundo shrugged.

"But if Carr was stalking Kristen, wouldn't the doorman have noticed?"

"I don't know," he repeated, more gruffly this time. Enough to intimidate her.

"Thank you for your help, Mundo," she said politely, as if she were a small child whose manners had been well taught. Something that did not come naturally. Not because she had been poorly brought up. But in the Fischman household sentences were never just six words long. And paragraphs usually went on for a few pages.

"What's this all about, anyway?" Mundo still sounded gruff.

"Um, nothing," Nina said. "I'm just trying to find out more about Mr. Carr for a project I'm working on."

Mundo turned to Howie. "Listen." He poked him in the chest. "I give you information because I know you a long time. But I don't want to read about my business in the papers. You know what I mean?"

"Oh no," Nina said quickly. "Nothing like that. You don't have anything to worry about." She gave Howie a "let's get out of here" look.

"Mundo," Howie said, "keep up the good work."

Nina wondered what he meant. Did he mean keep on giving us information? Or did he mean keep on fixing me up with good-looking young hookers? Or maybe he just meant keep on putting my mail in my box. Probably he didn't mean anything. Men said a lot of stuff that didn't mean anything. Like "yo" and "hey."

"Thanks again," Nina said as she started backing out of the mailroom. Howie followed her and they headed for the elevator.

"I told you," he said, when they were on their way up.

"What do you mean?"

"It's gotta be blackmail. Not only was Henry Carr banging

a prostitute, he was stalking one. I mean, in this day and age maybe you can't really blackmail someone for using a hooker. But stalking? Well, that's another story."

Nina immediately thought of Sol Wachtler, whose brilliant judicial career was ruined by such behavior. "You're right," she told Howie. "I mean, Henry Carr is anxious to get his name in the paper, but not as a stalker."

"Yeah, I imagine this is the kind of publicity he could live without."

The elevator opened on Jonathan's floor. Howie stepped out with her. "Thanks a lot," she said.

"So what are you going to do about this?"

"I don't know. Confront Carr?"

"He might be dangerous."

Nina laughed at the thought. "It's hard to picture him as a murderer. But I'll tell you one thing."

"What's that?"

"I had a job interview with him yesterday. This whole thing makes me think twice about working for him."

"Why? Afraid he'll stalk you next?" Howie made it sound like such a far-fetched idea that she felt momentarily insulted.

Nina reminded herself that there was nothing flattering about being the object of a demented sexual obsession. People knew that these days. In fact, the Napoleon complex had completely disappeared in the mental institutions, replaced by dangerous sexual fantasies about movie stars. Your average violent nut these days probably had only a hazy idea of who Napoleon was, but had no trouble believing that Jodie Foster was in love with him. And would kill to prove it.

Nina knew all this. But being with Howie made her regress, as if it were twenty years ago and she was worrying about now being cute enough to be stalked. "Thanks again," she said, and went back into Jonathan's apartment. His cat came out to see who had come home. "Remind me not to hang around with those kind of guys," she said to Sasha. "It's like throwing years of psychotherapy right out the window." Sasha started purring in what Nina could swear was an empathetic way.

CHAPTER 15

Nina didn't even have time to call Jonathan that day to check out his reaction. She had to run over to the office and draft an affidavit and then track down the client and get it signed and she was due at her sister's house for dinner that evening.

Laura and her family lived in Park Slope. Which was farther into Brooklyn than Henry Carr's neighborhood, but not so far that you really felt as if you were in a borough. Park Slope had a small-town feel to it, with a low skyline of three-story brownstones and people actually saying hello to each other on the street.

Ken, Laura's husband, had long wanted to put their brownstone on the market and head for the suburbs where he grew up. A brownstone had a certain charm, he said, but he was sick of living without a driveway. Laura didn't object to the suburbs on principle, but she had a long-standing fear of driving that had kept the family where they were. She had finally gotten her license last summer and Nina now wondered whether that would mean a move for the Rubin family. The two older kids went to Berkeley-Carroll and the baby was getting ready for nursery school. With three kids, private school tuition started to exceed the real estate taxes of a nine-room Tudor in Scarsdale. Nina had a suspicion that they might be Westchester-bound.

Nina usually met her mother on the Seventy-second Street subway platform and they took the IRT express out to Brooklyn together. Today, however, Ida had promised to baby-sit. The family's child care person was back home on some West Indian island for two weeks and Laura had to chair some committee meeting for the silent auction that the kids' school held every year. There was so much work involved, Laura said, that this was definitely the last year she would volunteer for the job. Nina couldn't believe that she actually had a sister who felt that doing charity work was too demanding. Nina had inherited Ida's genes, while Laura had inherited someone else's. But whose they were no one knew.

Nina used to think of Laura's house as beautifully decorated, but lately it struck her as a little fussy. Ever since the decade changed, the decor seemed dated. The floral bed linens, the golden oak furniture, the charming little jars of lemon curd and carrot jam all over the kitchen. Enough already, Nina yearned to shout. What this house needs is some plastic!

But Laura seemed not to notice that the Laura Ashley era was over. She continued to grow tea roses in the backyard and to clot cream in the kitchen. And to not work. Nina didn't think that Laura could ever work, she took so damn long to do everything. Nina understood that her sister did this in order to fill up her day. But in the process she had made herself unemployable.

The meal Laura served that night was also redolent of the eighties. The ingredients were of the annoyingly self-conscious variety. There were nasturtium blossoms in the salad and pink peppercorns in the sauce. Of course, it all tasted good, but was annoying nonetheless. Ken made fun of it all, but you could tell that he was into it. He went on and on about who had the best swordfish in the city. It turned out that he had bought the fish at Citarella, near his Central Park West dermatology practice, since he wasn't always satisfied with the freshness of the local offerings. After five minutes of that, Nina thought he had a hell of a nerve to make fun of a few nasturtium blossoms.

Most of the attention, when not focused on the salad or fish, was devoted to the children, who had various tales of birthday parties and soccer games. It seemed that nobody played softball or football anymore. Even the girls played soccer. Nina supposed that the injury rate was lower. And it had enough of a European connotation to make the parents happy, the parents being members of a generation who thought they had discovered goat cheese and the French cinema.

Dessert was modest, consisting of a bowl of some sort of orange things that looked and tasted like miniature persimmons but were apparently called sharon fruits. Nina was on her second sharon when she managed to get the conversation around to herself. "I had a job interview this week," she told them.

"No kidding," Ken said. "That's a historical event, isn't it?"

"I try to have at least one every decade."

"What kind of job were you interviewing for?" Ida asked.

"It was a staff position with the Public Advocate's office."

"What does the Public Advocate do, anyway?"

"I don't really know, Ma."

"Oh, I know him," Laura said. "Betty Carr's husband."

"How do you know Betty Carr?" Nina asked.

"From the Brooklyn Botanic Garden. We were on a committee together last year."

"That's right. They live in Brooklyn Heights."

"Most of her volunteer work is more Manhattany. You know, Junior League stuff. I'm sure she runs off to Madison Avenue every chance she gets. But she did help organize a fund-raiser we had last spring, at the tail end of the cherry blossoms. We called it Cheerio to the Cherries."

"Have you met her husband?"

"He was probably at the Cheerio thing. Let me think. Tall, graying blond, sort of good-looking without being interesting?" Laura might have inherited someone else's work ethic, but she still talked like a Fischman woman. At least when it came to describing men. "Interesting" was the family's favorite adjective.

"That's him."

"He's the one who interviewed you?"

"Uh huh."

"Well, the way Betty talks about him, he seems like sort of a joke."

"What do you mean?" Nina asked her sister.

"She's so contemptuous of him. She makes him sound like a screw-up instead of an important elected official. I'm always shocked when she talks about him like that. I mean, I don't know her that well. It's not like we're intimates. And you'd think that she'd be more discreet in public, considering his career and all."

"Well, I think he might be guilty of murdering Jonathan's doorman."

"Come on. No way."

"Why not?"

"Please, can you see that guy killing anybody?"

Nina had to agree. "No, not really. But I think that the doorman was blackmailing him."

"About what?"

"Some hooker."

ALTERNATE SIDES

"He was seeing a prostitute?"

"Well, he used to. Lately he had started stalking her."

"Stalking her? What do you mean?"

"According to the mailman—"

Ida interrupted. "Always the best source of gossip in a building," she said.

"Only if the doorman's dead," Nina responded. "Besides, it turns out that the mailman is a pimp."

Everybody said "What?" at once, except for Danielle and Jared, who said, "What's a pimp?" and Evan, the baby, who didn't say anything but was obviously trying to figure out why everyone was talking at once. So Nina launched into a long explanation about Mundo and Kristen and Ray and Henry Carr, adding for the benefit of the children that a prostitute was a lady who gave tea parties and that a pimp was her secretary, who kept track of her appointments and made sure that people paid her. Just like the secretary that Daddy had in his office.

"Well, I'd say that blackmail is a real possibility," Ida said. "I always wondered why no one ever blackmailed Sol Wachtler while he was running around torturing Joy Silverman. Someone must have recognized him in one of his disguises, creeping around the basement of her Park Avenue building. Don't you think?"

"Maybe someone was blackmailing him all that time," Ken said. "We'll never know. But, Nina, blackmail is one thing. Murder is another."

Then the children wanted to know what blackmail meant and Nina had to explain that it wasn't black or mail. That it was a kind of tip you give someone if they'd keep quiet and not talk. And Danielle said that Mommy had given them each a cupcake yesterday so that they'd go to their rooms and play without making any noise. And the cupcakes were

123

chocolate so they were black and was that blackmail? And Nina said she supposed it was.

"Ken's right," Laura said. "Blackmail is one thing, murder is another. Even if the doorman was blackmailing Betty's husband, I still can't picture Henry murdering anyone. Now Betty, she's another story."

"What's she like?"

"Complicated. Not a type I'm familiar with."

"I saw a photo of her," Nina said. "She looked a little flashy."

"Well, she's from Texas. So her hair's a little too big, her diamonds are a little too big. And she looks even flashier next to that Episcopalian husband of hers. Such a gray mouse. It's hard to imagine him consorting with prostitutes."

"But you read about that sort of thing all the time," Ida said. "Haven't you seen the statistics? Ninety-nine percent of the customers that the bondage and discipline people get are looking for dominatrixes."

"I didn't know you were such an authority," Ken said.

"Mommy, what's a domina—"

"Time for some more blackmail," Laura said. And sent the children upstairs with ice pops and a tape of *Aladdin.*

"Where were we?" said Nina, after the kids had left.

"Your mother was telling us about the bondage and discipline industry," Ken said.

"I was telling you about Betty Carr," Laura said. "I can see why her husband might resort to prostitutes. As I said, she ridicules him terribly. I get the impression that they married each other only because the other one had something to offer. In his case it was a prominent family and a promising political future. In her case it was money. Lots of nice shiny new Texas money."

"While his had gotten old and shabby?"

"I think it was wearing thin. And Betty wanted a different life. She told me that she was sick of the same stupid debutantes and oilmen. She came to New York on a shopping trip when she was in college. One lunch at Mortimer's and she was sold. She never wanted to go back."

"And how did she meet Henry?"

"She moved here when she graduated."

"And did what?"

"Volunteer work."

"I didn't know you could do volunteer work without being married," Nina said.

"What's that supposed to mean?" Laura sounded pissed.

Nina sensed that she was treading on dangerous ground. "No, really, I'm serious. I never heard of a young, single person living alone in New York and not having a job. Unless they're studying acting or painting or something."

"Remember, this was about twenty years ago. Before jobs were all the rage." Laura still sounded pissed. "Anyway, I'm sure she met him at some benefit or something. Or someone introduced them. She said she thought he'd be a senator by now. But he's turned out to be more limited than she predicted. And she's really annoyed at having to live in Brooklyn. She'd move to the East Side in a minute, but his political base is here."

"So if the doorman was blackmailing Henry Carr," Ida said, "do you think that his wife might be responsible for the murder?"

"Hmm." Nina and Laura both raised their eyebrows at each other.

"Because," Ida continued, "if her husband's stalking was exposed, it would mean the end of his career. Which would mean the end of everything that she moved here for. With a husband who's fallen into disgrace, and possibly even in jail, she might just as well pack up and go home to Texas."

"Except for one thing," Laura said.

"What's that?"

"I keep thinking that if Henry Carr was lying in the street with a broken leg, Betty would step right over him without breaking stride. If his political career was shattered, she'd divorce him, move to Manhattan, send the kids to boarding school and keep on lunching at Mortimer's and shopping at Bergdorf's."

"I didn't know that they sold Texas clothing at Bergdorf's," Nina said.

Laura smiled. "Yeah, her taste's a little off. She manages to find the most incredibly expensive ugly outfits."

"And that's not always easy," Nina said, thinking how great you could look if you were rich or thin. Especially both.

"Yeah, Betty's wardrobe is the classic waste of money. Anyway, I get the sense that she just doesn't give a shit about him. She managed to keep her hands on all the money. She has a prenuptial agreement, I suppose. So if she divorced him, she'd be just fine."

"Even so," Ida said, "wouldn't she be upset over a scandal? If only for the sake of the children?"

"Yeah, what about the children?" Nina asked.

"I don't know. She never talks about them. I'm not sure I even remember their names. There's a girl and a boy. Both are teenagers. One of them is named Berry, which is Betty's maiden name. But I can't remember if it's the boy or girl. The other one also has an androgynous name. Like Chapin or Whitney. It's the name of a hospital or school or something."

"Spence? Lenox? Browning?"

"Right, like that. But something else. I just can't remember what the child's name is."

"It doesn't matter," Nina said. "We get the idea. So do you think that Betty Carr is capable of murder?"

"I don't know if she's capable of actually killing somebody. Pulling the trigger and all that. But I think she's capable of arranging a murder. She's capable of arranging anything. She's a dynamo."

"Now, I don't think that arranging a murder is in the same league as arranging Cheerio to the Cherries," Nina said.

"You're all overlooking something," Ida said.

"What's that?"

"Assuming that the doorman was blackmailing Henry Carr, you still haven't established whether Betty even knew about it. Don't you think that would be a good place to start?"

"Good point, Ma." Nina turned to Laura. "So can you get me an introduction to Mrs. Carr?"

"I guess you could come to one of the meetings at the Botanic Garden. How do you feel about chrysanthemums?"

"One of my faves."

"Because Betty and I are both on next fall's Full Moon Mum Night. We've got a publicity committee meeting next week. I suppose I could sneak you in."

"That would be great."

"But I have a feeling I'll regret this."

"Don't be silly," Nina said. "I'll wear something floral. And I'll be so sweet that Betty Berry Carr won't even realize that she's spilling her guts."

CHAPTER 16

Nina and Ida rushed out before the dishes were cleared away. Their excuse was the subway, which wasn't great at eight and got really bad after nine. But the truth was that there was something about being in Laura's kitchen that neither was comfortable with. They could hold their own at the dinner table, but somewhere in the vicinity of the sink, they began to feel like handmaidens.

The Grand Army Plaza station was deserted enough to make them nervous, but a Number Three train came soon enough. It was filled with West Indian residents of Crown Heights and East Flatbush headed for Manhattan to do who knew what—clean offices, do the late shift in a hospital or nursing home, hang out and get drunk in a club or spend the night with a relative in Harlem. Their lilting accents served to counter Nina's usual nighttime subway fears. For a moment Nina pretended that she was on Barbados instead of the Seventh Avenue Express. But she knew what a week in the tropics in April would mean with her skin. A sure case of sun poisoning. So she let go of the thought and concentrated on what her mother was saying.

"Did you ever think of that?" Ida asked.

"Sorry, roll back the tape a bit. I didn't hear what you said. The woman next to me was telling her friend that she washes her rice eight times before she cooks it. How many times do you wash your rice?" she asked her mother.

"I don't wash my rice at all."

"That's not what they mean by dirty rice, Ma."

"My rice is not dirty. My rice comes in little cardboard containers from the Chinese restaurant. I just throw a little water on it the next day and put it in the microwave. Perfect rice every time."

"The next day, huh?"

"Sometimes the day after that."

"Ma, tell the truth. What's the longest you ever let leftover rice sit in its cardboard container before you ate it?"

"Oh, I don't know, I lose track."

"I must have gone a month."

"Is this a contest?" Ida asked.

"Forget it. Now, what were you saying?"

"About Betty Carr. You overlooked one possibility."

"What's that?" Nina asked.

"Well, you assumed that if she did kill the doorman, it was because he was blackmailing her husband. But maybe he was blackmailing her."

"I don't get it. Why would he blackmail *her*?"

"Because she stood to lose as much as her husband did if he was exposed."

"But Laura said . . ."

"I don't care what Laura said." Ida was adamant. "A woman with children doesn't just step over her husband's body and swagger on. No matter how lousy her marriage is. Besides, if it was common knowledge that she controlled the purse strings, maybe Ray the doorman went straight to her. Maybe Henry Carr didn't even know about it."

"I guess that's possible." She tried to imagine Jonathan's

doorman putting the squeeze on the woman in the photo in Henry Carr's office. How would he even approach her? It was hard to picture.

"How are you going to bring up the subject if you do meet her?" Ida asked.

"I don't know. I guess you can't very well walk up to someone and ask her whether she was aware that her husband was stalking a hooker."

"I've always found," her mother said, "that the best method for getting someone to spill their guts is to spill yours first. It breaks the ice."

"I don't mind breaking the ice with my guts. But what could I possibly tell her that's dramatic enough to get her to confess to murder? That I'm ambivalent about moving in with my boyfriend? That's not exactly hair-raising."

"How's that going, by the way?" Ida asked. "Now that you've raised the topic."

Nina gave her a dirty look. "You manipulated me into that, didn't you?"

Ida didn't respond. "Have you reached any conclusions?" she said.

"No." Nina turned away.

"You know, maybe the decision would be easier if you let yourself acknowledge how hard it is."

"Why should it be such a hard decision? What am I giving up? A small, crummy apartment in a walk-up tenement where the windows don't even close properly. And a life of unread *New Yorker* magazines and month-old take-out Chinese rice."

"That's exactly what I mean. Pretending that moving in with Jonathan should be the easiest thing in the world. And that you're a spoiled brat for not wanting to do it. It's a mistake."

"Why?"

"Because moving in means you'd be giving up a certain amount of independence. And you shouldn't pretend that doesn't mean anything to you."

"Independence? Is that what you call it? Starting to worry on Labor Day about New Year's Eve?"

"Nina, face it. You've always been able to do basically whatever you choose to do."

"Well, it doesn't feel that way. I don't know that I ever really chose to be a lawyer. Or to live in a crummy little apartment."

"You just wait until you have to start making some real compromises. Then you'll realize how much freedom you've had. And moving in is just the start. If you get married and have children, it all escalates to another level. Now you can see whatever movie you want. Once you have a baby, you can't even go to the bathroom when you want."

"I hate that. People with kids think that the rest of us are just all having the time of our lives. Like we don't have to worry about things like paying bills and getting constipated and falling on the ice."

"Nina, you know that's not how I think. All I'm saying is that moving in with someone is a big adjustment. And you shouldn't pretend that it's not."

Nina thought about it some more. What was she afraid of? She just couldn't picture never being alone. That was it. Being alone was such a big part of her life now. Giving it up would be like cutting off an arm.

"Maybe you're right. The thought of never being alone terrifies me."

"That's understandable. Besides, it's not like you're some teenager, moving out of your parents' house to get married. You've gotten used to a lot of solitude. And it's not easy to give up. Believe me, I love my solitude."

"You mean you're not pining away for the days when

your husband was alive and your kids were young and adorable and needed you every minute?"

"If I could do it all over again, I guess I would. But maybe I wouldn't. I enjoy my life as it is now."

The two women sat quietly as the train entered the tunnel between Brooklyn and Manhattan. It wasn't until it stopped at the Wall Street station that Nina spoke.

"So you think that someone like Betty Carr would pay off a blackmailer to save her husband's name?"

"Absolutely. You know what happens to the wives of disgraced politicians, don't you?"

"What happens to them?"

"They end up like Pat Nixon, living out their last years in New Jersey. And from what I've heard about Betty Carr, I don't think she'd enjoy living in New Jersey."

CHAPTER 17

Nina had been so busy thinking about her meeting with Betty Carr that she forgot all about her budding career with the Public Advocate's office. But on Monday she got a call from Carr's secretary informing her that Ed Kornbluth had a free hour or two and could she come in the next day. So here she was, back in the Municipal Building, wearing her good suit with a substantial portion of its hem taped up. She had meant to repair the skirt herself and then, having given up on that, had meant to take it to the tailor. But even that had proved too demanding and she resorted to Scotch tape. She had also been known to use staples, but only with loose weaves.

She had already worn this suit to her meeting with Carr, but it was really the only thing appropriate for an interview. All of her other outfits had that Legal Services look—a little too loose and a little too long. Her suit was cut closer and was an interesting shade of green. Which didn't do wonders for her skin tones, but made, she felt, a statement. It was a color that stupid people didn't wear.

She had shopped long and hard for shoes and panty hose in the right shades. Which wasn't easy when you wore queen-size tights and a wide-width pump. She had finally cobbled together the perfect combination of teal, sage and celery, but lived in fear of running the hose or ruining one suede shoe. Because she hadn't been able to force herself to buy extras and did not look forward to embarking on another exhaustive search.

Ed Kornbluth did not seem as if he would notice whether a person wore sage or aqua. He himself was also wearing green, a drab-colored suit that would have looked okay with a cream shirt and yellow tie instead of the white shirt and red tie that completed his outfit.

Prudence, Carr's secretary, had buzzed him when Nina arrived. "Eddie," she had said, "Nina Fischman is here." He seemed like the kind of guy that everyone would call Eddie. Fully grown New York Jewish men often still sported their childhood nicknames. Not in the way that WASPs did, with their Chips and Biffs. But by taking the first syllable of their names and sticking a "y" or "ie" on the end and clinging steadfastly for several decades, you had not only middle-aged Eddies, but also Bobbies and Richies and Howies. Nina had to actively resist the temptation to call him Eddie.

"Why don't you tell me a little bit about the office?" she asked, once she had settled in across the desk from Kornbluth. "I didn't get to discuss much with Mr. Carr."

"What did Henry tell you?"

"Well, we talked about Brooklyn Heights. And how it's changed."

"Ever live in Brooklyn?" he asked her. His New York accent was unmistakable. Eddie was not exactly movie star material. He was Mutt to Carr's Jeff, barely reaching Nina's modest five-and-a-half feet. He was probably around the same age as his boss, maybe a little younger, and had the kind of baldness that had recently been associated with heart attacks. His glasses had plastic frames and the lenses were a little smudged. No Occhiali Armani for this little fellow.

Eddie Kornbluth was the kind of guy who twenty years ago nobody would have wanted to go out with. But now that market conditions had changed, he had become the kind of guy who you went out with once and obsessed about whether to go out with again.

"I never lived in Brooklyn," Nina said. "But my sister lives in the Slope. I grew up in the Bronx."

"Well, Henry's a Brooklyn boy and I am too. Several members of the staff are. I don't know if we're prepared to take on someone from alien turf." He winked at her, not lasciviously, but to show he was joking.

"Yes, Charlotte's from Brooklyn, isn't she?"

"Oh, right, you're Charlotte's friend." He said it in an intimate way, as if Charlotte and he were members of the same team, kids who played together in the same treehouse. His life had probably always revolved around the office. Nina had a strong hunch that not only was he unmarried, but that he still lived with his parents.

"We used to work together."

"Well, Charlotte went to the same high school as I did. She was a few years behind me, of course."

"What high school was that?"

"Tilden."

So Eddie hadn't gone to Stuyvesant or Brooklyn Tech. Those were the specialized high schools, the ones you had to take a test to get into. If a Brooklyn boy went to a neighborhood high school, it meant either that he didn't get in or that his mother didn't want him to ride the subway. For girls it was a different story. Charlotte had gone to her neighborhood high school because in her day, Stuyvesant and Brooklyn Tech only took boys. The Bronx was a more enlightened place. Bronx Science had become co-ed not long after the war.

"Oh, Tilden. East Flatbush, right?" It was the kind of useless information that Nina prided herself on. Too bad they didn't have a category for New York City public high schools on "Jeopardy!"

"East Flatbush is correct." Eddie Kornbluth looked as if he prided himself on knowing the same kind of dreck. It made Nina nervous that most of the people she instantly related to were undeniable nerds.

"So how long have you been working with Henry Carr?" Nina had been on enough first dates to know how to get a guy going.

"A long time." He seemed relieved to be answering a question that referred to the past. Like his boss. "Henry and I go back about twenty-five years. I met him through the Flatbush Independent Democrats. He was just out of law school and I was in my senior year at Brooklyn College. He was running for City Council and he recruited me to do volunteer work."

"And he won?"

"No, but he ran again and won the next time. I've been working for him ever since."

She could just picture Eddie at the Flatbush Independent Democratic Club. Energetic and nerdy, perfect gofer material.

"He's always held some elected office? Ever since?"

"Except for a short stint as Koch's deputy mayor. But he found a place for me there too. I've never had to seek any other type of employment. Henry Carr has been my entire career." Eddie took off his glasses and held them up to the light, then wiped them on his tie. He looked sweeter with them off, almost cherubic.

"I see." It was a favorite first-date line of Nina's.

"It's funny, isn't it?"

"What's that?"

"If Henry Carr hadn't been born, I would have had an entirely different life."

And if he dropped dead tomorrow, Nina thought, you'd have to make some pretty substantial adjustments. Like a wife whose husband earned all the money and wrote all the checks. If Henry Carr died, Eddie would be more lost than Betty Carr.

Which gave Nina another thought. If anyone had a motive for keeping Carr away from scandal, it was Kornbluth. Guys like him just can't make the jump to the private sector. He was too much of a misfit to go corporate and without a graduate degree or family money, he'd be in trouble. Nina would bet that Eddie had neither.

So if Ray had been blackmailing Carr, Eddie would have gotten very nervous. Which put him right up high on the suspect list, along with Henry and the missus. Nina decided to probe a little bit further along these lines. "So what would you do if you came into work tomorrow and discovered that Henry Carr had decided to drop out and move to Maui and string puka shells?"

"Oh, Henry would never do that."

"How can you be sure?"

"He has his eye on Washington. And I think he'd run a good race. One thing though."

"What's that?"

"I don't know how his wife would feel about Congress."

"What do you mean?" Nina asked.

"I don't think she wants to leave New York. She says that the shopping isn't any good in D.C. And she's got her regular lunch crowd here that she'd miss."

"Oh, is she one of those ladies who lunch? Le Cirque, Mortimer's, that kind of thing?"

"Exactly." Eddie gave Nina a comradely look, to let her know that she shouldn't worry, he wasn't grouping Nina together with the Bee-yoo-tiful People. A look which she did not find at all reassuring. If she had to pick one side of the fence, she wouldn't necessarily opt to be put out to pasture with Eddie Kornbluth.

"So what about you?" she asked him. "How would you feel about a move to Washington?"

"Oh, I'm ready. I mean, I've lived in Brooklyn all my life. But I could go. The city's not what it was."

Here he goes, she thought, giving me the same rap as Carr. Except this time it's from the Jewish, lower-middle-class, East Flatbush perspective. And if these people, who were supposed to be safeguarding New York's good government, thought that the city was going to hell in a handbasket . . . well, then everyone was in big trouble.

"So you don't hold out any hope for turning things around?" she asked.

"We're doing what we can." Kornbluth put on his "Meet the Press" demeanor. "But as a watchdog agency, we don't really have the authority to make the profound changes that New York City needs in order to survive."

A watchdog agency. Nina pictured the staff of the Public Advocate's office chained to a doghouse, barking. Carr would be an Afghan hound, bred for long, fine bones and a pointy snout. Eddie would be a dumpy little mutt, scrappy and tenacious. And Prudence would be a poodle, a breed whose time has come and gone. Actually, the whole office seemed frozen in time, somewhere in the sixties, right before sex, drugs and rock and roll had got a firm toehold.

It was easy to imagine them back then—Carr with his lean jawline and a blue blazer, a young John Lindsay type making hearts throb. And Eddie, the earnest secretary of the Brooklyn College Political Science Club, in the image of Allard Lowenstein, complete with his heavy black eyeglass frames and sexual ambivalence. And Prudence, a newly married Vassar grad, timidly unpacking her china and crystal, taking French cooking lessons while waiting to get knocked up.

Most people had a peak year that they carried around with them for the rest of their lives. Certain details gave it away: the old ladies with the hennaed Rita Hayworth hairdos, the Elvis clones still patting their graying pompadours, the food co-op members clinging dearly to their threadbare flannel shirts. The Public Advocate's office seemed frozen in time thirty years ago, when "Independent Democrat" had a progressive ring to it. Before Ed Koch made the term into a euphemism for someone who just didn't know when to keep his mouth shut.

Could Nina be happy here? Part of that depended on whether any of the staff members had murdered her boyfriend's doorman. But putting that small detail aside, she still had her doubts. Thirty years ago, she had been a chubby, introverted schoolgirl, tortured by the hem lengths of the day. Life in the nineties was good. You could wear pants almost anywhere and long skirts came in all kinds of shapes —tulip, trumpet, pipe stem and flowing. Nina didn't want to go backward. Her peak year, she hoped, was yet to come.

"Well, as I already discussed with Mr. Carr, I feel like I have a lot to contribute to your office." As long as she was here, she might as well sell herself. She launched into an animated description of her press contacts and her ties to the elderly community.

Eddie Kornbluth listened carefully. He asked a few questions, all astute and relevant. He did not look out the window. He was clearly a highly developed political animal. He seemed to find Nina's answers acceptable, though he poked a few holes in her claims of media accessibility. But he did make her feel as if she might have something to offer after all. And she found herself getting enthusiastic that there could be life after Housing Court.

"Thank you so much for coming to see us," he finally said.

Nina knew that she didn't have to bother with a "you're welcome" for this guy. Not for someone who'd attended Samuel Tilden High School, who spoke the same vernacular as she did.

"Thank *you* for taking the time to see me, Mr. Kornbluth," she said, rising and shaking his hand. She turned to leave.

"I'll be in touch," he said. "And please do me one favor."

"What's that?" she asked, turning back.

"Call me Eddie."

CHAPTER 18

"Just one thing," Nina said.

"What's that?" Laura asked.

"Betty Carr doesn't know your maiden name, does she?"

"No, I'm sure she doesn't."

"Good. Just introduce me as your sister Nina. Don't mention Fischman, okay?"

"Why not?"

"Just in case all my investigating comes to nothing and the Carrs are innocent, I still want to preserve my option of getting a job offer from the Public Advocate's office. And I don't want Betty Carr mentioning that someone named Nina Fischman was nosing around her. It might make her husband suspicious."

"Okay. Whatever you say."

The sisters were on their way to the Brooklyn Botanic Garden. Laura had arranged for Nina to attend a committee meeting at which Betty Carr was supposed to appear. She was passing Nina off as an events consultant who had agreed to extend some help in planning Full Moon Mum Night. Nina thought that it would be easier to pass herself off as the President of the United States, since the only events she really felt capable of planning were simple ones, like eating lunch and making a phone call. But the meeting was supposed to be about publicity and Nina had to admit that she did have a certain facility for making sure that everyone heard everything right away.

Prospect Park had an early spring look of expectation. There were buds on the forsythia even though it was still mud season in Brooklyn. Like its Manhattan cousin, the park had a nineteenth-century feeling, as if Olmstead were putting the finishing touches on it. At times like this Nina considered moving out here, into a Victorian brownstone with oak parquet and refitted gaslight fixtures. But she knew that you really weren't supposed to live in Park Slope unless you were already planning two children and an ultimate move to Montclair, New Jersey. And she was planning neither at the moment.

She wondered whether Jonathan would like it in Park Slope. So far she had spared him an evening at the Laura Ashley Pavilion, since she didn't want to watch Ken cross-examine him about his employment history. But maybe she'd take him for a test drive out here. Brooklyn might provide a good resolution to the "my side of the park" controversy that had Nina and Jonathan at such a standstill.

Nina had worn what she hoped could pass as a committee-woman outfit, complete with a hat. Hats had become big this past winter and young women who at another time might have produced hand-painted silk camisoles or started an upscale cookie company were now becoming milliners.

Nina had forced herself to buy one. She liked the idea of them, but felt foolish actually putting one on. The truth was that black women always looked fabulous in them, while white women often looked like buffoons. Her hat was black velvet and resembled a chocolate cake sitting on her head. She wasn't really sure that this was the kind of hat that women wore to Tuesday afternoon committee meetings and she was becoming more self-conscious by the minute. She'd consider taking it off, but where do you hide a seven-layer hat, anyway?

Betty Carr was not wearing a hat. She couldn't have worn a hat, since her hair was up in some tousled beehive arrangement, as if she were trying to look like Brigitte Bardot. Or maybe she was trying to look like Ivana Trump and it was Ivana who was trying to look like Bardot. In any case, her suit was exquisite, with a long fitted jacket and pants so slim they had tiny vents in the cuff so you could pull them over your feet. And the color was pretty, a deep cobalt, more sophisticated than navy and red, but still wrong. The effect was just too loud for the Brooklyn Botanic Garden, the color too artificial in comparison to the muddy shades on the rest of the women. She stuck out like an empty potato chip bag in the bushes.

The committee chair had phoned to say she'd be late, so while the rest of the women schmoozed, Nina and Laura made a beeline for Betty. "So good to see you again," Laura said, squeezing her elbow.

"How are ya?" She still had a Texas accent and her voice was a little louder than the rest of the ladies. She had a hearty exuberance that you normally didn't see in this town. Nina almost expected her to slap Laura on the back.

"Betty, this is my sister. Nina, this is Betty Carr."

"Hello."

"Hello." Betty's hello was louder.

"I asked Nina to come and help us with some publicity ideas. She's a genius when it comes to such things."

Nina shrugged. She waited for Betty to cross-examine her, to say in her loud hearty voice "Oh yeah? A genius in what way?" But Betty just smiled and thanked her for coming. Years of having bitchy lunches with women who were too mean to eat had not diverted Betty's natural urge to be polite.

Nina wished she had come up with a more detailed game plan. How was she going to get this woman to talk about her husband's bad habits? It seemed impossible. She was going to have to take radical action. Actually, she had an idea.

"I almost didn't come today, but I'm glad I did," Nina said, giving Laura a look she hoped served as a sufficient warning to keep quiet. "I need the distraction. You see . . ." she dropped her voice to a mumble, ". . . I'm going through a rather difficult divorce."

Nina figured that was guaranteed to get Betty's attention. She was right. Betty's eyebrows arched up in a "tell me more" expression.

"Men! I can't believe they're not extinct yet." Nina tossed her head, thereby sending her hat flying. She retrieved it, but decided not to put it back on her head. She held it awkwardly for a moment, until Laura gently took it and placed it on a chair.

"Poor thing," Betty said. "It must be awful. Do you have any kids?"

"No. I'll be all right. My friends have been really great and I have my job and all. But I just feel so . . . I don't know . . . so *trite*. I mean, if you're going to get divorced, it should be for a more interesting reason than your husband cheating on you, don't you think?"

"I guess so," Betty said.

"The thing of it is . . . oh, never mind. I shouldn't be shooting my mouth off like this, should I?" she said to Laura.

"Whatever makes you feel better," her sister said.

"I suppose you're right. Talking is so cathartic. If only men knew that, they wouldn't drop dead of heart attacks so early."

"Absolutely," Betty said, laughing.

"Well, the truth of the matter is that he wasn't really cheating on me. Not exactly. What really happened was that I found out that he had been frequenting a prostitute."

Betty got a wary look on her face, as if she didn't know whether she was being set up. Nina knew that the next line she spoke was critical. It could pull Betty Carr in or send her fleeing.

"A prostitute. Can you believe it?" Nina said. "I mean, it's so old-fashioned. And you wouldn't think," Nina continued, "that in his field he would have to pay for it."

"What field is that?" Betty asked, still wary.

"He's a college professor. He's surrounded by adoring, nubile young things, all anxious to give it away. Power in the classroom is a strong aphrodisiac. I mean, the only other group of people that gets it for free as much as professors are politicians."

"Watch out, Nina," Laura said. "Betty is married to a politician."

"Really?"

"Yes, Henry Carr, the New York City Public Advocate." Her sister gave a convincing performance, sounding both embarrassed and amused.

"You know what I think?" Betty asked.

"What?"

Betty leaned over to whisper in Nina's ear. She smelled about eighty proof. Nina realized that alcohol, rather than Texas, might account for her hearty exuberance. "It could be worse."

"In what way?" Nina asked.

"At least it's grown women he's running around with. Think about all those men consorting with little boys and girls. Like that lawyer from Cravath who they found dead in a Bronx motel last year. Killed by a teenage male hooker. I can't remember his name but I've met his wife. A really nice woman. They live somewhere on Park."

Nina remembered the incident. "David Schwartz," she said.

"Right. Schwartz. And what about that guy who tried to have his wife killed in a New Jersey shopping center so that he could run off with a Korean prostitute?"

Nina also remembered that incident. "Robert Goldberg," she said. "He was a real estate executive."

"Right. They were both respectable members of the community. Either of us could have been married to either of them."

"David Schwartz, Robert Goldberg, yeah, I must have gone to high school with at least one of them."

"So you should thank your lucky stars that your husband hasn't taken out a contract on you."

Nina smiled a little, then screwed her face up into a tortured scrunch. "But you see . . ." she said, taking Betty's arm and going in for the kill, ". . . I can't help thinking that it was something I did. Or didn't do. That good wives don't have this happen to them."

"Let me tell you something." Betty pulled her arm away and put it on her hip.

"What?" Nina had a feeling that she had struck pay dirt.

"It has absolutely nothing to do with what kind of wife you are. These men go to whorehouses for reasons that have nothing to do with you. They find those women gratifying and uncomplicated in a way that a wife could never be. Believe me, I know."

"How did you find out?"

"What do you think I am, an idiot?" Betty snapped. "How did *you* find out?"

"I see your point," Nina said meekly. "It's not that hard once you decide to open your eyes."

"The important thing is not to blame yourself."

"I guess you're right." Nina sighed. "I feel better, I really do. Thank you for, you know, opening up to me. I appreciate it. And don't worry, I won't tell anyone what you told me. I understand that you're in a delicate position, with your husband's job and all."

"Ha." Betty threw back her head. It was more of a whinny than a laugh. "My husband's job is not paying our bills. That's another thing to remember, honey. Don't ever let yourself get into a position where they could take you down with them."

"But how do you protect yourself?"

"For one thing, don't let him get his hands on any of your assets, just in case you've got to dump him in a jiff. In my marriage there's his, mine and ours. And mine is mine and ours is his. Get it?"

"But a marriage is more than assets. Don't you find his infidelity emotionally upsetting?"

"I've gotten used to it. But things get sticky at times. Like when someone spots him and reports back to me. That's always embarrassing. And I do worry that he'll end up in the papers or being blackmailed or something. But then I just tell myself that no matter what happens, I'll be okay."

Nina wondered whether this was all just bravado. And whether this woman could have just gone through the terrorizing ordeal of being blackmailed because of her husband's behavior. But Nina didn't think so. Maybe Betty Carr was being a little too cavalier, exaggerating her indifference. But she truly seemed to consider her husband's infidelities to be mere annoyances, as if he had run up too big a telephone bill last month.

Besides, there was no reason for her to spill her guts to Nina about Henry Carr's whoring, even if she was a little drunk. If this was a woman who had killed a blackmailer to make sure that her husband's reputation remained intact, she wouldn't be likely to blab such details to a total stranger.

Unless Betty was on to her, unless she knew exactly what Nina was doing and why she was doing it. Nina felt as if she had done a credible job in portraying the distressed, wronged wife. But maybe Betty Carr had seen right through her and decided to call her bluff. Anything could have given Nina away. For one thing, she now realized that she wasn't wearing a wedding ring. And even though she claimed she was in the middle of a divorce, it might still have made Betty suspicious.

Nina would have to ask Laura what her impressions were. But that might not be worth much. Laura's observations were uneven. She was brilliant when it came to predicting whether some guy would ever call you again. And right on the money in deciding whether to keep or discard specific items of clothing. But she didn't always bother to read between the lines, to interpret the subtext. Nina doubted whether Laura had been listening to Betty on two different levels. But then Laura didn't have to. She lived a life that presented itself on one lovely level. Her sister wasn't someone who needed to be mucking around in the basement of other people's thoughts.

"You were brilliant," Laura said.

"Thank you. But I had help."

"What do you mean?"

"She was drunk."

"I wasn't talking about Betty. I was talking about your suggestions for publicity. Inviting the Japanese ambassador was a great idea." The sisters were walking down Eastern Parkway, Nina to the subway and Laura back to her house. The meeting had proven to be interesting, Nina thought.

She had no idea that chrysanthemums had such a long and complicated history. "But I was just bullshitting," Nina said.

"Well, that's what publicity is. Bullshitting. And I think you have a real talent for it."

"Thanks, I guess." Maybe Laura was right. Nina had gone into law partially because it seemed like bullshitting could get you by. Unlike science, where you really had to know something. And bullshitting had served her well in Housing Court. But law required bullshitting according to a set of complex, arcane rules. While the meeting she had just sat through was pure fun. No arcane rules. You just tried to think up a good idea and then told everybody about it. And they all told you how clever you were and someone else ran off to implement it. You didn't have to sit around thinking how to phrase it in the correct jargon or do hours of boring research to see if there was any precedent for it. It had been her dream since she was a child—a job without homework.

Could working for Henry Carr be like this? It seemed to her that the main thrust of what would be required was publicity-related. This might be her chance to get out from the oppressive yoke of the law. Maybe public relations was really what she was born to do. Nobody had ever even heard of it back in the Bronx she had grown up in, unless it was the whisper of a juicy item into Walter Winchell's ear at the Stork Club. Certainly no one considered it a career for a person like Nina.

"What did you think of Betty Carr?" Nina asked her sister.

"I told you before. I think she's a little nutty."

"But did you believe what she was saying?"

"She seemed pretty convincing," Laura said.

"The problem with people like Betty is that it's hard to see through what they're saying to determine objective reality. Because they truly believe everything they're saying.

They're so convincing that they convince themselves. So it's not as if they're lying. It's more like the truth has very little to do with what they're saying. Do you know what I mean?"

"I guess so. I also get the feeling that she's pretty moody. An idea will hit her and she'll go on and on, and then she'll forget all about it. And when you bring it up again, she'll ask you whatever are you talking about."

"Well, some of that might have to do with her drinking," Nina said. "Is that a common thing with her?"

"It's not the first time I smelled alcohol on her breath."

"Well, what did you think about what she said? About the content, not about the veracity."

"You mean all that stuff about not letting him take you down with him?" Laura asked. "And protecting your assets?"

"Yeah, that stuff."

"Well, as you know, I have no assets."

"Right," said Nina. "I recall that our father's estate consisted of outdated periodicals and a few items of clothing that were showing decades of wear."

"So as far as protecting myself financially," Laura said, "I did not consider her advice to be relevant. As far as protecting myself emotionally, that's a harder question. Why are you so interested in this anyway?"

Nina squirmed a little. "Well, I thought it might be something I should give some consideration."

"There are no absolute truths when it comes to marriage, you know. Everyone's so different. Look at the two of us, for example."

"I know we're different," Nina said. "But which particular difference are you talking about?"

"Nina, I don't think that financial or emotional vulnerability is going to be your particular issue in your marriage.

You're just not the kind of person who is going to put all her eggs in her husband's basket.''

"What makes you say that?"

"Look, someone like me, who married young, who has no long-standing intimacy problems . . . well, I'm another story."

Nina felt herself getting defensive. By having no long-standing intimacy problems, she wanted to say, what do you mean? A tendency to become totally dependent on another human being? But she kept her mouth shut.

"But you," her sister continued, "you'd be more likely to keep all your eggs in your own basket. And peck your husband's eyes out if he came near them."

"That's a nice thought. It has all the right images—cold, selfish, bitch, and so on. Thanks a lot."

"I don't mean that you're any of those things. I just think that people who have an easy time letting someone into their lives, do so. And those who don't have an easy time, don't. And so far you haven't."

"It's not as though there's been a long line of suitors, you know. Most of the men I've gone out with mysteriously moved to Cleveland the next week."

"But here's one who hasn't. And look how nervous you are," Laura said.

"What makes you think that I'm nervous?"

"For what other reason would you be screaming?"

Nina exhaled deeply. "I am screaming, aren't I?"

Laura nodded.

"I am nervous, aren't I?"

Laura nodded again.

Nina looked at the arch that loomed ahead at Grand Army Plaza. It was impressive, even if it was only an imitation of the one in Paris. The arch was certainly grander than the one planted in Washington Square. "It's like sleep-away camp," she said. "Sometimes I used to get so homesick that I never thought I'd make it through the summer. And I didn't want to work it through. I didn't want to analyze the underlying reasons. I just wanted to go home. And that's how I feel now. I don't want to do the healthy thing and forge ahead. I just want to get into my nightgown, crawl into my bed and stare at my own ceiling for the rest of my life. Alone."

"That doesn't sound so bad to me," Laura said.

"Come on, you wouldn't trade. Not for a minute."

"For more than a minute. For a whole weekend, in fact. A long one. I haven't seen my ceiling in quite some time."

"You'd miss the kids."

"I'd get over it."

Nina had always assumed that everyone was lying when they told her how good she had it. That all those family types were pretending to envy her freedom, while secretly pitying her. While she was sure that there was a genuine element of pity and contempt, Nina was starting to think that some of the envy was also genuine. That some of these people weren't just internally gloating, but really were depressed or angry or regretful.

So if people like Betty Carr, or even Laura, secretly felt as if they'd rather be single and childless . . . well, it made Nina wonder what she was getting into.

CHAPTER 19

Nina gave Jonathan an edited version of her trip to
the Brooklyn Botanic Garden, going light on Betty's views of
marriage. And she didn't bother to mention the follow-up
conversation she had with Laura on Eastern Parkway.

"So you like the life of a society matron?" he asked.

"Yeah, it was fun. More fun than going to work. At the
office, if I have to sit in a two-hour meeting, it's because
somebody's going to get evicted or some grandmother is going to lose custody of her grandchild. What's the worst that
could happen at the Botanic Garden? Full Moon Mum Night
isn't as successful as they hoped and they won't be able to
expand their bonsai collection this year."

"It didn't seem like a waste of time?"

"Not really. I think I could get used to living a life with no
downside."

"I don't think that anyone really feels that way," Jonathan said.

"What about your mother? You said that she cares more
about her rose garden than anything else."

"She's human. She has the same fears that we all do."

"Like what?"

"Cancer. Violence. Aphids."

Nina hadn't met his mother yet. She knew it was going to be painful and she wanted to make sure that it wasn't going to be pointlessly painful. Jonathan had described her as the kind of Jewish mother who wanted her son to marry a Protestant. And Nina was a far cry from a Protestant.

"You know who we should pay a visit to?" he said.

Oh no, she thought. Please let me get a haircut, get my teeth cleaned, lose five pounds and lose my accent first. And become Protestant and terminate therapy. I'm not ready to meet your mother. "Who should we pay a visit to?" she asked.

"Kristen."

"Kristen?" His mother's name was Marjorie.

"You know, the hooker on the twenty-sixth floor. That Carr has been stalking."

"Oh, yeah, Kristen," she said with enormous relief.

"She might have some idea of what was going on between Carr and Ray. Besides, if you're seriously thinking of working for the Public Advocate's office, wouldn't you be interested in talking to the woman he's been stalking?"

"I thought of that," Nina said. "But I was afraid she'd charge us for her time. Besides, the whole thing seems sort of awkward."

"Well, it's not your everyday situation, but she's probably used to strange things happening in her line of business. Maybe she'll join us for a cup of tea."

"What are you going to do? Just go up to the twenty-sixth floor and knock on her door?"

"No, I'm going to call Howie and find out her last name. Then I'm going to look her up in the phone book and give her a call."

"What if she's not listed?"

"Then I'll go upstairs and knock on her door."

"I have a better idea," Nina said. "Let's have Howie call her. And come with us."

"Why?"

"I think it'll be smoother. He already knows her, so it won't be as weird."

"All of a sudden you're shy?"

"I've always been shy. I've just been overcompensating for it over the past several decades. Besides, what if we go up and knock on the door and she's with a client?"

"Then she probably won't open the door."

"I think we should call Howie," she insisted. She didn't know why she was finding the idea of talking to Kristen so intimidating. But it was. Nina didn't think she had ever met a prostitute. She had probably never even met anyone who later turned into a prostitute. Even the worst skanks at Bronx Science went to graduate school.

"Okay, you're so attached to the guy, you call him." Jonathan sounded a little jealous.

Nina was flattered. She considered explaining to him that guys like Howie were never interested in women like her, but her good judgment took over. She enjoyed the rare occasions when that happened.

This time she remembered Howie's last name and got him on the phone right away. She explained their mission. "Do you have her phone number?" she asked.

"Yeah, I do."

"You mean, it isn't like you call Mundo and Mundo calls her and then she calls you?"

"No. I just call her when I want."

"So what's to prevent the two of you circumventing Mundo?"

"I don't know."

"That's the same problem they have in the temp agencies."

"Look, I don't know." He sounded annoyed. Also embarrassed. "I guess she's afraid of him so she cuts him in."

"Anyway, could you call her and see if she's available? If it's not too much trouble."

"No problem."

"And then could you come with us? I think she'd probably feel more trusting if you were there."

"Okay. I'll call you right back."

"Thanks." Nina hung up.

"The police left a message on my answering machine," Jonathan said.

"You're kidding. When?"

"This morning. After I left for work."

"Why didn't you tell me?"

"I just did."

"What did they want?"

"They were checking to see if I had any new information for them. If I did, I should call them."

"Did you?"

"Did I what?"

"Call them?"

"No, I just got the message."

"What are you going to do?"

"What do you think I should do?"

"Well, all this stuff about Ray calling Henry Carr and your mailman being a pimp and Carr stalking your neighbor, who happens to be a hooker . . . I guess it qualifies as new information, doesn't it?" Nina chewed on a cuticle.

"I guess it does."

"And we haven't shared any of this with the police as of yet, have we?"

"No, we haven't."

"Why haven't we?" she asked.

"Because I think that on some level we still believe we're imagining the whole thing."

"Maybe you think so, but I don't."

"So how come you haven't called the police?" he said.

"I'm just not ready yet."

"What are you waiting for?"

Nina shrugged. "I don't know."

"You're just a control freak."

"I'm not a control freak," she protested. "Control freaks hate flying. I love flying. I love the fact that I can't do anything about what's going on and if the plane goes down no one can blame me. That's not the behavior of a control freak."

"Then how come when you overhear someone giving directions in the street you have to interrupt and give better directions?"

"That has nothing to do with control," Nina said. "It's just a desire for accuracy. And an impulse to be helpful. Besides, most people give crummy directions. It's not my fault if I have a superior knowledge of the New York City transit system."

"So what should I tell the police?"

"I don't know. Let's decide after we talk to Kristen. Maybe things will become clearer."

"Or maybe we'll forget that the police ever called," Jonathan said.

The phone rang. "Yeah, it's more fun this way, isn't it?" she said, and then listened to Howie telling her that Kristen could see them right now.

CHAPTER 20

Kristen looked a little haunted, though everything seemed neat and tidy around her. Her blondish hair was in a tight French braid, with only a few escaped wisps. Her cats seemed polite and well nourished and there was hardly any feline hair on her couch. There were African violets on the windowsill, brimming with blooms and devoid of dead leaves. The air smelled of a spicy potpourri that sat in a crystal bowl on the coffee table, the kind that had an open-work metal cover to let the scent through.

Kristen could have been Little Suzy Homemaker, except for a haunted and hard look in her eyes that spoke of a past that no doubt included mobile homes and a drunken stepfather and all the other horrors that plague little white trash girls who are too pretty for their own good. She was living the legacy of Tonya Harding and Norma Jean, and Nina couldn't help but worry about what would ultimately happen to her.

Nina could also tell that Howie and Jonathan were not dwelling on the psychodramas contained in Kristen's past and future, but instead were concentrating on the fact that she was a spectacular physical specimen. Her French braid was thick and long and streaked with gold (although it remained unclear whether the gold was honestly come by). Kristen had a long, thin, graceful body, more Nancy Kerrigan than Tonya Harding. And she showed it off with an outfit that could have been a skating ensemble. Her body was clad neck to wrist to ankle in black Lycra, covered by a slinky red garment that might be a dress or might be a vest, depending on how liberal you were.

Nina was so preoccupied with imagining Kristen's childhood as a young abused girl in a Kansas trailer park that she almost did a double take when Kristen finally opened her mouth and emitted a stream of pure Noo Yawkese. "Hi, Howie. Howya' doin'? Didja get rid of that awful cold yet?"

"Yeah, I'm better. Kristen, this is Nina and Jonathan." They all nodded and smiled at each other. Tiny little nods and smiles, the way New Yorkers do.

"Sit down. Wouldja like something to drink?"

"No, we're fine, I think," Howie said. Nina and Jonathan gave tiny little nods of assent and sat on the couch.

"We appreciate your taking the time to talk to us," Nina said. After all, somebody had to prod the conversation past the tiny little nod stage.

"No problem." Kristen curled into a chintz-covered armchair and Howie sat down in a nearby rocker.

"Howie, tell Kristen about our conversation with Mundo." Nina suddenly felt too self-conscious to use the word pimp or prostitute or stalking.

Howie must have felt the same way, because the narrative he launched into was filled with "you knows" and "likes" and shrugs. "So Mundo said that he wasn't going to, uh, you know, like do business with Carr anymore because he'd been following you around and bothering you. Is that what happened?" he asked Kristen.

She pushed a wisp of hair back into her French braid.

Then she examined her fingernails, which were chiplessly polished. She had the kind of nail job that the salons call a French manicure and charge extra for, clear with white at the tips. Understated and classy. "It's a long story," Kristen said, looking from Howie to Nina to Jonathan.

Nina wanted her to make it even longer. Start at the beginning and explain why someone who looked like a Midwestern farm girl had a borough accent. And then tell how she had gotten into this line of work. And how she kept her hair so neatly braided. Whenever Nina attempted a French braid, it ended up looking like a clump of tumbleweed had blown in and somehow attached itself to her scalp. These were questions Nina wanted answers to, but had little hope of getting.

"How long have you known Henry Carr?" Jonathan asked.

"About two years."

"Mundo sent him?"

"Yeah. He became a regular. Every Wednesday, late afternoon. Like clockwork. I think he told everyone he had a weekly squash game, because he used to use my phone to call people and pretend he just got off the squash court."

"Did he seem like a weirdo at first?" Jonathan was still asking the questions.

"No. He liked to be dominated. But almost all these guys do. Nothing too heavy or violent. No bondage. Just a little shouting and stamping my foot. And a little pinching."

"Pinching?"

"Yeah, he liked to be pinched."

"Okay." Jonathan paused.

Nina jumped in. "So when did he first start giving you trouble?"

"Well, after about a year of Wednesday afternoons, he started telling me that he loved me."

"So what did you do?" Nina asked.

"I told him that I loved him too."

"You did?"

"Well, he was an excellent client."

"I see."

"Then he started calling during the week. At first it was just now and then. But it became more frequent until he was calling me several times a day."

"What was he saying?"

"He said he couldn't live without me and that he would leave his wife for me."

"Did you encourage him?"

Kristen shrugged. "As I said, he was an excellent client. And Mundo told me not to blow him off. So I tried to be friendly and professional without encouraging him. But then he started slipping notes under my door. And calling me and demanding to see me. He'd want me to drop everything on a moment's notice. And with my schedule that's impossible." She uncurled her legs and crossed them. "You know I also work two days a week for my uncle. In Jersey."

"Your uncle?"

"He's an optometrist," Kristen hurriedly explained. "I'm the receptionist."

"Why do you work there?"

"For the health insurance."

"You're kidding."

"I need health insurance, just like everybody else." Kristen sounded huffy.

"Are you from New Jersey?" Nina asked.

"Nope. Brooklyn. Bay Ridge."

"Oh." So that explained her accent. And maybe her bone structure too, because Bay Ridge was an old longshoreman's neighborhood and still had a substantial Norwegian population. Kristen must have sprung from the same gene pool as half of Minnesota. Maybe she spelled her name Kristin, which seemed more Scandinavian. There had been no name on the door, just a blank space over the bell. Nina tried to see if there was any mail lying around that might give a clue, but none was in view. The room was too tidy for mail.

"So after a while," Kristen (or Kristin) said, "it wasn't just notes and phone calls. He started following me around. I'd be taking a dance class and I'd look out the window and he'd be down on the sidewalk, watching. Or I'd come out of the PATH train on the way home from my uncle's and he'd be sitting across the street in a coffee shop. I'd always pretend that I didn't see him and he'd never come over to me. It was really creepy. Then he started getting into disguises."

"Disguises? Really?"

"At first it was just something like a rain hat pulled low over his eyes or a collar turned up. But then he got more outrageous, putting white powder in his hair and pasting on a mustache. Once he even went to all the trouble of renting a postal uniform and following me around in it."

Nina immediately thought of Mundo when Kristen mentioned the postal uniform. Was there some sort off sick conspiracy going on between Carr and Mundo? "How do you know that the uniform was rented and not borrowed?" Nina asked.

"He told me later. When I asked him about it."

"You confronted him?"

"I had to. The whole thing was getting ridiculous."

"You weren't afraid?"

"Look, in my line of work, there are always incidents. Henry was by no means the worst. I've had guys beat me up, leave urine-filled condoms on my doorknob, lock me out in the hall without any clothes. Men seem to think that abuse goes with the territory."

"Did you ever consider working for your uncle full time?"
Nina asked.

"When I'm older, I'll go get a regular job. But for now
. . . well, you can't beat the money. If I go work for my
uncle I'll be living in some crummy garden apartment in
Jersey, driving a Fort Escort, shopping at Lerner's and dating
guys who work in pizza parlors."

Nina was pretty sure that Kristen would never have to
date guys who made pizza. She was good-looking enough to
date men in the Donald Trump league. Or at least in a minor
Trump league. But Nina understood what she meant. Fate
had handed Kristen a difficult hand to play. She was too
good-looking to be a receptionist, but did not have quite the
right look for modeling. And with that accent, acting was
out of the question. There wasn't going to be any money
that was as easy as hooking.

Although most would consider the analogy strained, Nina
felt the same way about being a lawyer. She was fluent and
literate in a way that made it a waste not to practice law.
Although there wasn't anything about law that she really
liked. And, like the oldest profession, abuse came with the
territory. But why be compulsively articulate in front of the
classroom for twenty dollars an hour when you could do the
same in front of the courtroom for thirty? Nina knew she
would make an excellent schoolteacher, but who could afford to teach?

"I'm sure you'll never have to date anyone who works in
a pizza parlor," Nina said. "And if you do, it'll be the head
chef at Spago."

"I don't know about that." Kristen checked her nails
again.

"So what we're trying to figure out," Jonathan said, "is
the relationship that Henry Carr had with Ray, our door-

man. Because Ray called Carr before he died. And we don't know why."

"You don't think that Henry killed him, do you?" Kristen asked.

"We don't know what to think."

"Henry couldn't kill anyone. Not if his life depended on it."

"How can you say that?" Nina asked. "With such unpredictable behavior, dressing up in disguises and all. Clearly he was a bit of a meshuggeneh, if you know what I mean."

"Putting on a postal uniform is not the same as shooting somebody in the head. Henry might have been a nut, but he wasn't a violent nut."

"So why would Ray have called him the week he died?"

"It probably had something to do with me," Kristen said.

"With you?"

"Yeah. I mean, somebody had to be putting those notes under my door. It was either Henry, after Ray had let him into the building. Or Ray himself, carrying out Henry's request."

"Do you think that Henry was paying Ray for his cooperation?"

"Definitely. We all know that Ray would have done anything for money." It was a strange thing for a hooker to say.

"Did you ever see Ray and Carr together?"

"Sure. Sometimes, if I was running late, Henry would wait for me in the lobby. And he'd be talking to Ray when I got home."

"That's funny," said Jonathan, "because Mundo didn't say that he ever saw them together. Maybe Mundo had finished with the mail by the time Carr got here."

"No way." Kristen cut her hand through the air for emphasis. "I've seen the three of them standing around in the lobby, shooting the shit."

"Are you sure?"

"Absolutely. Mundo knew damn well that Ray was helping Henry get to me. They were all as thick as thieves."

"Pretty strange, huh?" Nina looked at Jonathan. He nodded.

"Did you ever talk to Ray about his little conspiracy with
Carr?" he asked Kristen.

"Sure." She nodded. "I'd say 'Ray, gimme a break. Keep
that guy out of the building. He's driving me crazy.' "

"And what did Ray say?"

"He'd tell me how much Henry loved me. And I think he
believed it."

Nina thought about it. It all seemed so unbelievable, except when you remembered that the Chief Justice of the
New York State Court of Appeals had dressed up as a cow-
boy and mailed condoms to Joy Silverman's teenage daughter. Nina had seen Wachtler once at a state function in Al-
bany. He had delivered an after-dinner speech. Although he
seemed quite charming, she had thought something was
wrong with him at the time. Too much hair dye and too
little nose for a sixty-year-old Jewish guy.

Henry Carr didn't indulge in hair dye or plastic surgery.
And Nina wondered whether she would have pegged him as
a nut if she had never heard of his stalking problem. His
romantic fixation with the Brooklyn Heights of his youth
could have been an indication of imbalance, or it could have
been the same sort of spiel that anyone sitting on a random
subway train on a random Tuesday afternoon would have
indulged in. Everyone missed the past. Except for Nina,
who, upon carefully inspecting any chapter of her life, was
invariably glad it was over.

"Do you think it was possible that Ray was blackmailing
Henry Carr?" she asked Kristen.

"How could it be? They seemed so friendly."

"What about Mrs. Carr?" asked Nina.

"What about her?"

"From what I've been told, Betty Carr controls most of the money in that family."

"She controls everything in that family," Kristen said. "The money is the least of it."

"Well," said Nina, "do you think that Ray could have been blackmailing Mrs. Carr? And that she could have been paying him to keep quiet in order to protect her husband's career? And Henry didn't even know about it?"

"I doubt it."

"How come?"

"For one thing, according to Henry, she always had one foot out the door. She'd probably use attempted blackmail as an excuse to get a divorce."

"Did she know about you?"

"I don't know if she knew specifically about me, but she sort of got the idea."

"But she didn't use that as an excuse to get a divorce?"

"No," said Kristen, "she seemed to think it was normal."

What kind of family did Betty Carr grow up in, Nina wondered, if she thought this was normal.

"Another thing," Kristen said, "is that I don't think that she considered Henry's career worth protecting. She seemed to have a lot of contempt for what he did. She kept saying that he'd never go anywhere."

"Even after he was elected Public Advocate?"

"Especially then. She had been hoping he'd leave government and become a banker like her friends' husbands."

"Was there anybody else who really cared about Henry's career?" Nina asked. "So much so that Ray could have blackmailed them? Someone who worked with him, for example?" She wondered if Kristen had ever met Eddie Kornbluth.

"Look, I don't really see Ray as a blackmailer."

"Why not?" Nina asked.

"He was interested in money, but I think he planned to take another route."

"Like what?"

"I don't know. I mean, as far as I could tell, he was a money-grubbing little pig and he'd have ratted on his best friend for ten dollars. But he was so eager to please that it was disgusting. There's a word for it, but I'm not sure what it is."

"Unctuous?"

"Sounds right. He'd never have the balls to look someone in the eye and say 'Pay me or else.' You two have lived here for a while, haven't you?" She turned to Jonathan and Howie.

"Yeah," they both said.

"So what do you guys think?"

"I think you're right," Howie said.

"I think you're right, too," Jonathan said.

Which left Nina without any suspects. Unless Kristen wasn't telling the truth. Maybe Henry Carr wasn't really so innocuous. Maybe he was really scaring the shit out of her. And Ray was helping him. And maybe Kristen had gotten really pissed off at the two of them. And killed Ray. And maybe Carr was next.

It was, thought Nina, an improbable scenario. But it kept at least one person on the suspect list.

CHAPTER 21

"So what did you think?" Jonathan asked Nina.
Howie had gone home to watch a basketball game.

"At first I thought that she was from the Midwest. Until she opened her mouth. She was really good-looking. Maybe she could model, except for something about the lower half of her face. I don't know exactly what it was. A slight weakness of the chin, perhaps. What did you think?"

"I wasn't talking about how she looked. I was talking about what she said." Jonathan pulled off his Rockports and put his feet up on his couch. "For Chrissakes, Nina, it was your idea to run around investigating this murder. Now you can't even stay on the topic."

"Well, I just met my first prostitute. I'm all excited. It's not what I pictured, with those African violets and chintz all over the place."

"Did you think that she was telling the truth?"

"Well, I thought a couple of things."

"Do you ever think just one thing?" he asked.

"Do you want to hear what I have to say or not?"

"Go ahead."

"First of all, do you think that she spells her name K-R-I-S-T-E-N or I-N?"

Jonathan looked at Nina as if she were crazy. "I don't know."

"Because if she's from Bay Ridge, she could be Norwegian. Especially in light of the fact that she's a blonde. And I think that Scandinavians spell their names ending with I-N. Like Isak Dinesen."

"That's E-N."

"But her real name was Karin Blixen."

"That's also E-N."

"But the Karin is I-N. Or maybe it is K-A-R-E-N. I'm not really sure."

"I think that this conversation has nothing more to offer," he said.

"But maybe Kristen's Irish and I'm wrong about the I-N. Do you know her last name?"

"No, I don't." Jonathan was at the eye-rolling stage by now.

"Do you mind if I check her mailbox? Just to see. I'm too curious to concentrate on anything else until I resolve this."

"You can check her mailbox, but if you do, it'll be on your way out."

"Okay, okay. Never mind." Nina was manic, the way she got when she crossed paths with another human being she couldn't quite figure out. She tried to picture the exact moment that Kristen had decided to become a prostitute. Had it something to do with a friend who had already been there? Or a boyfriend who knew someone? Or maybe she was a runaway. Did you count as a runaway if you were from Brooklyn? Nina supposed you could get off the N or R train at the Port Authority as easily as you could take a Greyhound in from Milwaukee.

"Besides, I already checked her mailbox," Jonathan said.

"You did? When?"

"Yesterday. I was curious."

"So what's her last name?"

"I don't know. It was blank, like her door. Kristen didn't believe that Carr was capable of murder. Or that Ray was capable of blackmail. What do you think?" he asked.

"Well, you knew Ray better than I did. What do you think?"

"I did have a thought." Jonathan opened his palms. "It's just a thought. Kristen says that Ray wasn't capable of blackmail. I don't know about that. Maybe she's covering something up."

"Like what?"

"Maybe Ray was not only blackmailing Henry Carr, but he was also blackmailing Kristen. And she was the one who had him killed."

"That's ridiculous," Nina said. "Who would bother blackmailing a hooker?"

"Why not?"

"In order to be a proper target of blackmail, you have to have something to lose. Like Carr did. What does Kristen have to lose?"

"Well, she could get arrested," Jonathan said.

"So she gets arrested. Prostitutes get arrested all the time. They hold them for a couple of hours and then give them time served. They never seem to take it seriously, at least in the movies."

"Maybe he could have threatened to tell her family."

"Really, how much could he have gotten out of her? I mean, she had a nice apartment and all. Her cats were purebreds and her upholstery was expensive. But I doubt if she's worth big money."

"Maybe not," Jonathan said.

"Think about it. It's never the call girl who goes down in a scandal like this, it's always the politician. Think back. Who took the hit—Profumo or Keeler?"

"Profumo?"

"Right. Old Christine Keeler just made a fortune giving interviews to the tabloids. I mean, why would Kristen pay Ray to keep his mouth shut? If the media got wind of the fact that Carr was stalking her, she'd probably just sell her story as a mini-series or something."

"I guess you're right."

"What I thought," Nina said, "was that maybe Kristen was pissed off at Ray for helping Carr to stalk her, so she had him murdered."

"That's even a lamer theory than mine."

"Maybe, but where does all this leave us? There aren't any suspects left." Nina noticed that she was starting to whine.

"Well, I might not be able to indulge in any investigative activities for too much longer."

"Low frustration tolerance?"

"Uh . . . no. Actually, I have a situation developing at the office . . ."

"Big deal," Nina said. "So you came in late one morning. They're hassling you about that?"

"That's not what I'm talking about."

"Uh oh." She was worried.

Jonathan had been between jobs when Nina had met him. It wasn't unusual in an industry as volatile as the advertising business. He was an illustrator and they were the first to get dumped when the agency lost a client. But he had brooded the whole time he wasn't working and seemed convinced that he'd never find another job. It was only since he'd started at his present agency that they began to discuss moving in together. Nina didn't want to go through another unemployed period with him. "What's going on?" she asked in what she hoped was a supportive and gentle manner. But she wasn't always a good judge of her own voice.

"They're probably going to send me to L.A. for a year." Nina saw her life flashing before her. Her face turned bright red and there was a buzzing in her ears. This was the worst news imaginable, short of illness, death and destruction.

"Los Angeles?" She practically wept. "I don't want you to go to Los Angeles."

"Well, you can come with me. Would you like that?" He put his arm around her shoulder and pulled her close to him.

"I don't want to go to Los Angeles. What am I going to do there?" L.A. was a hopeless place. If she wanted to be someplace where people wore shorts she'd make aliyah to Israel.

"I don't know. We could move in together out there. It would solve our fight about which side of the park to live on." He smiled at her and smoothed her hair.

Suddenly her aversion to the Upper East Side seemed small and trivial. Like a resident of Sarajevo fussing about which wallpaper to put up. She'd give anything to stay right here, in 10028, in this building with the smoked mirrors and the mailman pimp and the hooker who had a way with African violets. In light of Jonathan's news, it all seemed quaint and charming. Even the doorman with a bullet in his head leaking blood onto the front seat of her boyfriend's Volvo.

Because compared to what life would be like in southern California, a corpse seemed like a minor irritation. Unknown horrors awaited her out there. She had been there once and the pain had blurred her memory. But she had vague recollections of everything she hated—nondeciduous trees, skimpy clothing and weather that made your thighs rub together. The worst thing had been that all locomotion—both vehicular and pedestrian—seemed to take place on wheels. Teeming packs of joggers circumnavigating the Central Park reservoir was bad enough. Rollerblading, however, was completely intolerable.

Besides, here in New York she knew how to play to her strengths. Out in L.A., she wouldn't have any.

On the other hand, could she just let Jonathan pack up and leave? Nina believed that marriage was often a matter of timing. People got married because they were in the mood. And if Jonathan was in the mood, he'd find someone else in California.

She reminded herself that a mere few days ago, she was telling her sister that she wanted to lie in bed, alone, staring at her ceiling for the rest of her life. So why was she already feeling jilted?

She loved him, she supposed. At least she felt deeply attached to him. But did he make her bubble over? Was he the kind of guy she just couldn't stop talking about? Did she steer the topic of conversation around so that she could mention him in every breath whenever possible? No on all counts. She liked being with him, making love to him, cuddling up to him at night. But when she slept alone in her own apartment, did she ache, did she pine, did she long? No again.

She thought back to some of the achees, pinees, and longees that she had consorted with in the past. The pine state had always been short-lived and the objects of her affections had all taken on a cartoon-characterish persona in her memory. Would she trade Jonathan in for one of those loony tunes? No. Was she ready to start dating again? No. Was she ready to give up men? No. Was she ready to move to Los Angeles? No matter how hard she tried, the answer was still no.

If you answer no to every question, she told herself, you

fail the test. If it was anyplace other than Los Angeles, she might be able to move. Someplace crisp and invigorating like Toronto. Or wholesome and craftsy like Bennington. Or exotic and alluring like Bangkok. Or even frumpy and stuffy like Philadelphia, where she could at least nurse her contempt. But L.A. was the worst, a place where people looked down on you before you got to look down on them.

"What do you think?" Jonathan asked.

Where do I start? she thought. "Oh God, I don't know," she said.

"Don't you think it could be kind of fun? You wouldn't have to work, because the company's paying for my housing."

"Oh, great," she said. "I could just Rollerblade all day."

Jonathan removed his arm from her shoulder and put his head in his hands. And then it struck her. He was truly upset. He cared about her. This was a new experience for Nina. Oh, she was sure that men had cared about her in the past, in a vague and anaesthetized way. Once in a while they had even told her that they loved her, although they always sounded as if they were more concerned with trying to convince themselves than with convincing her. But no one had ever put his head in his hands before.

Nina felt a tug. The tug was halfway between her stomach and her shoulder blades, a part of her body that she had never been tugged at. The tug spread to an ache that climbed up her throat and clotted into a lump. The lump shook off tiny little beads of moisture that filled her tear ducts. There was a small amount of spillover.

"The California bar exam is murder, you know," she said.

He lifted his head up and looked at her miserably. "We're only talking about a year."

"That's what they're telling you now," she said. "But just

wait. They'll suck you in and never let you go. You'll spend your middle age living in fear of earthquakes."

"What am I supposed to do? Quit?"

Nina didn't know what to say. It had taken him a long time to find this job. "No, don't quit. Let me think about this."

"You know I'm not going to be any happier out there than you would," he said.

She didn't know if that was true. He looked better in shorts than she did. Jonathan also had a strong tendency to hop in his car when he had nothing to do, which would serve him well in California. When Nina had nothing to do, she'd hang around the new releases table at Shakespeare's and then wait on the fish line at Zabar's. And maybe visit her mother. All of which would be hard to do in L.A.

But how happy was she going to be buying fish on Broadway without him? Not very. She'd always rather be with him than not be with him. It occurred to her that this is what people meant when they said they were in love. Besides, he made her laugh and he made her come. What more did she want?

"Let me think about this," she said again, this time more softly. She pulled his face close to hers and traced the creases in his forehead with her middle fingers. She kissed his nose, then his mouth.

They sank into each other and then, as a couple, sank into the couch. Nina erased her mental blackboard and let sex take over, in the same way that sleep descends. Los Angeles would still be there tomorrow. In the meantime, she was feeling a different ache, the delicious kind that comes from genital engorgement. She might as well get laid while she still had the opportunity.

CHAPTER 22

Nina was on a double date. A triple date, actually, depending on your method of calculation. Jonathan and Nina were meeting her sister and brother-in-law and they were all going to an evening of fun and festivity at the Brooklyn Botanic Garden. Laura had claimed that Betty Carr would be there with Henry in tow. Nina thought that the event would offer a good opportunity to observe husband and wife and what went on between them.

So there they would all be—Nina and Jonathan and Laura and Ken and Betty and Henry. There were so many subplots going on that it gave Nina a headache.

For one thing, Laura and Jonathan had never met and Nina was nervous. She found herself scrutinizing him in a certain detached way, checking for flaws that she had never even considered before. Not a bad physical specimen, she thought, watching him bend over to lock the door of his car in front of her sister's house. He was a little broad in the beam, but his gray pinstripe hid it well. Nina had spent her life hating men in suits and everything they stood for. But now she had to admit that they were a brilliant invention. The suits, of course, not the men.

Jonathan was tall and fair and still had all his hair. And possibly someone else's too, since it tumbled down his forehead and mixed in with his eyebrows. It was the kind of hair you would call blond if you were a New York Jew. Once he got to L.A., however, he'd be instantly transformed into a brunette.

L.A. was another subplot that was being played out. Nina was refusing to discuss it. This was uncharacteristic of her. She normally did not resemble Scarlett O'Hara in any conceivable way. She did not have an eighteen-inch waist, nor did she think about things tomorrow. She thought about things immediately and endlessly, obsessing into the night. But L.A. kept getting elbowed out of the way. She just didn't want to deal with it, although it was eating holes in her unconscious.

She did not want to move to Los Angeles, nor did she want Jonathan to move there. It was as simple as that. There was no cure for this situation. And she couldn't help feeling as if she had brought this all on herself, by not appreciating what she had. She should have picked herself right up and moved into Jonathan's apartment the minute he had suggested it. If she hadn't been such an ungrateful wretch, maybe her karma would have been purer and this never would have happened.

It was funny, Nina thought, that it wasn't until Jonathan had announced that he was moving to another coast that she saw fit to introduce him to her sister.

As they climbed the steps of her sister's brownstone, Nina watched anxiously to see what Laura would think of him. But the person who came to the door was Ken. She knew what Ken would think of him. Jonathan wasn't Ken's kind of guy. Ken liked those regular Long Island kind of guys. Not ones like Howie, who were divorced and worked for their uncles and did business with prostitutes. But ones like Ken's partner Joel Slotnick, who had straight teeth and thin wives and a good rim shot. And a thriving practice (either medical, dental, law or financial planning) didn't hurt.

And Ken wasn't Jonathan's kind of guy. Jonathan was uncomfortable around men who talked endlessly about investment properties and tax implications and how their overhead was killing them. And a thriving practice didn't help.

"Hi, Ken. This is Jonathan." The two men shook hands. Nina noticed with some satisfaction that Jonathan was the taller of the two.

"Is Laura ready?" she asked.

"I'm almost ready," Laura called from the top of the stairs. She had one shoe on. She held the other in her hand. It was a beautiful shoe, a brown and beige high-heeled T-strap. The strap was made of braided leather. Laura's dress was orange, a color that used to be so undesirable that its status was automatically elevated to hot. Laura managed to look pretty good in orange. Her strong dark coloring actually looked good in most shades.

When the Fischman sisters were little girls, Nina's fair complexion and blue eyes seemed enviable. After all, it was a time when Doris Day set America's pigmental standards. But now it just seemed like a head start to skin cancer. While Laura, with her black eyes and dusky skin and generous nose, looked more like the ethnic models that the fashion industry had begun to use.

And gray looked dramatic against Laura's dark brown. Her isolated white strands made her hair look like one of those spin art paintings that kids brought home from street fairs. Nina's gray, on the other hand, blended into her light brown and made it look . . . well, if not exactly mousy, at least like some other kind of drab mammal. Squirrely, perhaps.

Nina had worn a pair of wide black velvet pants and a silk

jacket that was meant to be sort of flashy. But she hadn't achieved the desired effect. The jacket was the color of Nina's hair (or, even worse, Nina's hair five years from now). Nina had thought it understated and sophisticated at its point of purchase, but now it reminded her of something a Shaker might wear. She had tried to tart it up by wearing a black lace camisole under it, but the neckline of the jacket was cut higher than she remembered so a mere inch of lace showed, not enough to reverse the Shaker effect. Her shoes were as high-heeled and provocative as Nina could manage, which meant they came from the Nine West Spa Collection.

Laura put on her other shoe and came down the stairs. "You must be Jonathan." She took his hand.

"We finally meet," he said.

"How are we getting there?" Laura asked.

"My car's double parked outside."

"Isn't that nice." Laura fidgeted with an earring. It was brushed gold, and dangled, ending in a downward pointing arrow made of green-colored glass. Earrings all seemed to have sprouted points a few years ago and many were still hanging off fashionable earlobes.

"What's it doing out there? Raining?" Ken asked.

"A cold drizzle," Jonathan said. "Button your lining back in."

"And I thought spring had sprung."

" 'April is the cruelest month.' "

"I hear ya'." Ken went into the front hall closet.

I hear ya'? Was this her tight-assed brother-in-law the dermatologist speaking? It was as if he and Jonathan had been transported to the basketball court.

"Where are the kids?" Nina asked.

"Watching television, of course," Laura said. "The sitter will be here any minute. Want to come up and see them?"

"Sure." That was the thing about brownstones. Everything took place on separate floors. In order to change rooms, you had to climb a staircase. It was such a commitment. Nina preferred just being able to drift from room to room without thinking about it, the way she lived the rest of her life. Although her apartment offered limited drifting opportunities. "Jonathan, want to meet the kids?" she asked.

"Okay," he said, and followed her up the stairs.

Nina always found children particularly adorable in pajamas, ever since she first saw the nursery scene in the Mary Martin version of *Peter Pan*. And here was the updated version of Wendy, John and Michael. But instead of an English sheepdog, they had a Peruvian guinea pig. Laura had forbidden the family to get a pet whose turds were bigger than your standard Kalamita olive.

"Aunt Nina!" Evan, the baby, was always the first to run over. The older two took a while to peel themselves off the television screen.

After hugs and kisses all around she introduced them to Jonathan, not forgetting Esmeralda the guinea pig.

"That's an unusual name for a guinea pig," he said to Danielle, who was almost nine and big enough to wear a nightgown.

"It's a Spanish name," Danielle explained. "She's a *Peruvian* guinea pig."

"Wanna hold her?" Jared asked at the top of his lungs. He was six and had a tendency to yell instead of talk. He also had a tendency to kickbox instead of sit still.

"I'd be honored," Jonathan said. "I've never held a *Peruvian* guinea pig before." Jared plopped Esmeralda onto Jonathan's lap and Evan toddled over to watch. Jonathan managed to get Esmeralda to perform a small ballet *en pointe*, which cracked the boys up. So far, Jonathan was really doing well with the males in the house. Danielle, however, was reserving judgment.

"Daddy makes her do the twist," she said, clearly unimpressed.

Jonathan made the guinea pig gyrate. " 'Let's twist again, like we did last summer,' " he sang. " 'Let's twist again, like we did last year.' "

Danielle seemed to be won over by the little fluffball doing a Chubby Checker routine. "Do you have any pets?" she asked Jonathan.

"I have a cat, but she's not as good a dancer as Esmeralda."

"I want a kitty, but my mother won't let me have one."

"Well, you can come over and play with Sasha if you like."

"Where do you live?"

"In Manhattan."

"Do you live with Aunt Nina?" Jared asked.

"No, you silly," Danielle said. "Aunt Nina lives *alone*." She gave the last word a much less glamorous reading than Greta Garbo had.

Maybe she *should* move to L.A., Nina thought. Even an eight-year-old could tell that there was something unusual about living alone. They could move to L.A. and buy a guinea pig of their own. Or maybe, in light of Sasha the cat, a different kind of small mammal would be preferable. A child, perhaps.

Having a baby seemed unimaginable. But then so many people did it. It was as she had told herself during the bar review course—if her stupid cousin Bruce could pass the bar, she could.

She tried to picture herself with a child in Los Angeles, but all she kept thinking about was how sunburned both of them would get. It would only be for a year, she reminded herself. She pictured herself pregnant and sweaty, giving birth in a hospital that she would have to drive on a freeway to get to. And then sitting in an air-conditioned house, worrying that the baby was getting cold air blown on it. And taking it out into the backyard and then worrying that it was getting heatstroke. And having to put it in a car seat every time she wanted to go somewhere.

She had waited almost forty years to have a baby. If she was going to have one, it was going to be in Mount Sinai, thank you very much, and she was going to wheel it around Riverside Park.

Here she went again. It was the same routine as not wanting to live on the Upper East Side. If she kept on with this kind of shtick, she might as well go out right now and buy a Peruvian guinea pig because she'd sure as hell never have a child.

Nina picked up Esmeralda and cuddled her. She was a very sweet little thing, but an inadequate baby substitute. "I do live alone," she said to Danielle. "But I'm thinking of moving to California with Jonathan. What do you think about that?"

"My friend Erin moved to California. She goes to Disneyland all the time. When are you going to get married?"

"I don't know." Nina turned red.

"Why don't you get married on my birthday? It's soon."

"When is it?" asked Jonathan.

"May twelfth."

"Okay. Do you want to get married on May twelfth?" he asked Nina.

"Yeah, I guess."

"You can get married at my birthday party." Danielle was being very generous. "Do you want a rabbi or a judge?"

"Boy, you know all about this wedding stuff, don't you?" said Jonathan.

"Three of my friends got to go to their fathers' weddings

this year. One had a rabbi and two had a judge." She looked at Jonathan closely. "Are you Jewish?" she asked.

"Yes."

"Then you can have a rabbi."

"Do you want a rabbi?" he asked Nina.

"Yeah, I guess." It was the only thing she could think to say under the circumstances.

"The sitter's here. And if we don't leave soon, we're going to be late," Laura called from the hall. Then she popped her head into the room.

"Mommy, Nina and her boyfriend are getting married at my birthday party. Is that okay?"

"Sure." Laura looked at Nina but didn't say anything.

"So we'll need two cakes," Danielle said. "A birthday cake and a wedding cake. And then they're moving to California. So can I go visit them and visit Erin too?"

"You'll have to ask Aunt Nina."

"Can I, Aunt Nina?"

"Yeah, I guess." Nina was in a verbal rut and it was getting her into big trouble.

"What was that all about?" Laura asked once they were in the car.

"Danielle proposed to us," Jonathan said. "And we accepted, didn't we, Nina?"

Nina stopped herself from saying "Yeah, I guess" again. "Not only did she propose to us, but she set the date," she said.

"She's been wanting a wedding in the family very badly," Laura said. "All of her friends' parents are getting married for the second time and I think she's a little jealous. She's been marrying off everything she can get her hands on—her dolls, her brothers, her baby-sitter, even the guinea pig."

"Well, I'm sure that Esmeralda made a lovely bride," Nina said.

"What's this about California?" Laura asked.

"My agency's sending me to L.A. for a year," Jonathan said. "Needless to say, Nina's not thrilled."

"Are you going to go with him, Nina?" Ken asked.

"Well, I sort of told Danielle that I would. So I guess that I am."

"You sound like it's a jail sentence," Ken said. "I think it sounds great. Aren't you tired of the subways and the slush and all this gray? Don't you want to see some real colors?"

"Not really."

"What would you do about your job?" Laura asked.

"I don't know. Request a leave of absence. Quit if I had to. They'd probably take me back."

"And would you work while you were out there?"

"I don't know. I'm sure I'd have a hard time finding a job."

"Why don't you just relax?" Ken waved his hands around. "Swim. Hike. Play tennis. Do all those things you can't do here."

Nina considered explaining to her brother-in-law about how she'd planned her life around never having to wear shorts. And how disruptive this California thing was.

Nina tried to shut out all thoughts of shorts and get a feeling of cheerful optimism going. She was getting married. Of course, she had drifted into it in the most ridiculous way. But that was the way she did everything. Nina wasn't a one-two-three-go type of person.

"Well," Nina said, changing the subject, "I can't wait to see the Carrs in the same room. Although it's hard to picture them together. They make such an odd couple, don't you think?"

"Umm, they might not be there," Laura said.

"What do you mean?"

"I sort of heard something yesterday about Betty being in the hospital."

"What do you mean 'sort of heard something'? Is she in the hospital or not?"

"Uh, yeah, she is."

"So if she's in the hospital, it's not very likely that she'll be waltzing away the evening at the Brooklyn Botanic Garden, is it?"

"I guess not."

"Laura, what were you thinking? You know I only dragged Jonathan out here because the Carrs were supposed to show up. Why didn't you tell me they weren't coming?"

"I only found out yesterday. Besides, I thought we might have fun."

"This was just a trick so that you could lay your beady little eyes on my boyfriend, wasn't it?"

"Look, Nina, it would have been stupid for you to have been in the same room with Betty and Henry at the same time. She'd remember that you were the woman who told her that you were going through a divorce and he would have said that he had interviewed you and didn't you say that you were single."

"I didn't tell him that I was single. You know, it's against the law to ask a prospective employee about their marital status. It presents potential for employment discrimination."

"Then she would have asked you why you didn't tell her that you had just interviewed with her husband. In any event, they would have figured out that something screwy was going on. You're better off this way."

"Better off driving around Brooklyn in the rain to attend some stupid dinner with a bunch of dim-witted charity ladies? No offense, I guess. But what a waste of time."

"It's not really raining, Nina," Jonathan said gently.

"Only a drizzle. And maybe it will be fun. I'm actually glad that we came."

She supposed he was right, that the evening wasn't really turning out to be a waste of time. After all, she had, for the first time in thirty-nine and ten-twelfths years, managed to get herself engaged to be married.

CHAPTER 23

The first person to call her in the office the next morn-ing was not Nina's mother. Although she was sure that message unit would be spent shortly. But when the phone rang it was Charlotte Klein, Nina's friend who worked for Henry Carr.

"How are you?" Charlotte asked.

Nina considered launching into a long narrative about Los Angeles and her May wedding, but the reality of the night before had faded. By now, Nina couldn't be sure it had all really happened. So she just said "Fine" and left it at that.

"How are you?" Nina asked.

"Okay."

"I hear that Carr's wife is in the hospital," Nina said.

"Word travels fast. How did you hear that?"

"My sister knows her. Through the Brooklyn society matron network. That is, if being married to a dermatologist can make you into a society matron."

"Only in Brooklyn," Charlotte said. "Listen, I have good news for you. Eddie Kornbluth is crazy about you."

"I'm seeing someone."

"Don't be silly. I mean that he wants to hire you, not date

you. Actually, I'm not sure where he spends his romantic passions. Probably on his *Mad* magazine collection."

"Yeah, he seemed like the *Mad* magazine type."

"The funny thing is that he used to have this really lovely girlfriend. She seemed perfectly normal—pretty, smart, nice. And she wanted to marry him."

"You're surprised?" Nina said. "Don't you know that under present market conditions, women like us have to date men like him."

"So how did you find someone?"

"Just luck. A fluke, like hitting the lottery. Well, maybe not that much of a long shot. More like winning at Sunday night bingo when you're playing with four cards. You know, I've been looking for a long time."

"Haven't we all?" Charlotte sounded defeated, bordering on depressed. "I keep feeling as if I should buy a few more bingo cards. Maybe run another personal ad or go to Club Med or something. Where did you meet him?"

"Fire Island."

"But I've already done that. I can't go through that share thing again. I think I'd rather join the army."

Charlotte Klein was the kind of woman who made liars out of all those therapists who told their patients that there were great men out there, that it was just a matter of attitude. Nina had known Charlotte for a long time and had seen her try this and try that and be open and available and all that crap. And go out with man after man, none of whom was good enough for her. And overlook their shortcomings and she still got dumped all the time. Because there wasn't a thing that all the therapists on the West Side of Manhattan could do for her. The problem was that Charlotte Klein was not attractive.

Nothing terrible, mind you. No harelip or facial scars or bald spots or anything. But she just didn't look good enough to compete in a market where the odds were against her. Actually, Nina often thought that Charlotte was kind of cute in a dumplingish sort of way. She was small and round, with a round hairdo, round eyes and a cute little rosebud of a mouth, sort of like Betty Boop. But dumplings just didn't cut it in this day and age, even if they had replaced the egg roll as the Asian appetizer of choice.

"Anyway," Charlotte said, "Eddie really liked you. I think he wants to hire you."

It was time to mention Los Angeles, that much was clear. "What's wrong with Betty Carr?" Nina asked instead.

"I think she's having a hysterectomy or something. She has bad fibroids. But do you want to hear about Betty's uterus or your prospective employment?"

"How long has she been in the hospital?"

"I don't know. Jesus Christ, are you looking for a new job or not?"

"I might be . . ." Nina tried to launch into an explanation about California but Charlotte cut her off.

"Of course you are. You've been hiding out in that office long enough. Legal Services isn't a life sentence, you know."

"I'm thinking of moving. Out of the city, I mean."

"There's no need to go overboard. There's something between Legal Services and a commune in Vermont. Anyway, Eddie wants you to meet Margaret."

"Who's Margaret?"

"Margaret Connell. If Eddie is Henry's right nut, then Margaret's his left."

"Does Henry want to hire me?"

"Henry will do whatever Eddie and Margaret tell him to do. So you're supposed to come in next Wednesday. Is that okay?"

"Yeah, I guess." It was the same line Nina had used when

Jonathan proposed to her. Or whatever it was that he had done.

"What time is good for you?"

Nina checked her calendar. "Anytime. I'm not in court that day."

"Shall we say ten o'clock?"

"We shall." It was typical of Nina, never being able to say no to anything. She hated to delete any potential plot developments from her internal script. Even if it meant saying yes to a new job in New York, getting married and moving to California all at the same time.

"And stop by and see me when you're here," Charlotte said. "Last time you were in and out without even saying hello."

"Okay, I will." It had seemed childish to go searching for her friend in the middle of a job interview.

"So who is this guy?" Charlotte asked. "The one you met on Fire Island."

"Jonathan Harris. Very sweet. He's not a lawyer. He's in advertising."

"Has he moved in?"

"No. He lives on the East Side. He'd rather I move in with him, but I've been resisting it."

"How come?"

"At first I thought it was just this block I had about the neighborhood. You know, he lives in one of those high-rises on Third Avenue. Totally characterless. I just couldn't see myself there."

"But you could see yourself living alone in your dump forever?"

"Umm . . ."

"I don't mean to offend you," Charlotte added quickly. "But from where I'm sitting, your reluctance seems pretty demented. I mean, the last man I got fixed up with had a prison record. And you're complaining about Third Avenue?''

"Well, I did agree to move to California with him," Nina offered as some sort of defense.

"You wouldn't move across the park, but you'd move across the country?"

"Yeah. Pretty silly, huh?"

"So what happened?"

"What happened with what?"

"What happened with California? How come you're not moving?"

"I am. I think."

"So why are you looking for a job in New York?"

"I just thought I'd keep all my options open." Suddenly Nina felt like an option pig.

"Nina, Eddie is ready to hire you. Unless Margaret absolutely hates you, he's going to make you a job offer. Which means that you're going to have to turn him down. Or else change your plans to move. It's as simple as that. You can't have it both ways, you know."

"But I never have it any way. I've been sitting in my apartment for thirteen years, sitting in my office for the same damn thirteen years, going out with jerk after jerk. And now all of a sudden everything's changing and I have to decide what to do. And I can't deal with it."

"Well, deal with it." Charlotte didn't sound like the warm little dumpling she usually was. She made Nina feel whiny and infantile. "So do you want to cancel the interview?" Charlotte asked.

"No, no. I really haven't decided about California. I might not move if I got this job."

"Does Jonathan know this?"

"He knows me. So he knows how ambivalent I am about everything. He's got to expect that anything could happen."

"Hmf." It was more of a snort than a word.

"So tell me," Nina said, changing the subject in a desperate attempt to avoid further disapproval, "what's Margaret Connell like?"

"She's interesting." Charlotte let Nina hang for a while. After all, Nina knew that just because Charlotte was short and chubby didn't mean she had to be nice all the time. "Margaret's older than us," Charlotte continued. "Very direct. No nonsense, no bullshit."

"What should I wear?"

"I don't know."

Charlotte must really be pissed, Nina thought. It was a question calculated to get almost any woman going, but Charlotte wasn't biting. Nina didn't blame her. Charlotte had gone to all the trouble of talking Henry Carr into interviewing her and Nina was acting like an ungrateful wretch, planning on moving to California and not even letting Charlotte know.

But even so, Charlotte was going a little overboard. Nina couldn't help but feel that there was some jealousy involved. This was a side of Charlotte that she had never noticed before. She had been thrown off by the Betty Boopness of her. Could Charlotte have been involved in Ray's murder? Nina supposed it was possible, considering that this previously unrevealed edge she was showing was sharper than expected. It could be a complicated office conspiracy—Carr, Eddie, Charlotte, even Margaret Connell might be involved. They all had something to lose if Carr went down.

She'd keep this in mind at her interview on Wednesday. In the meantime, she'd continue to avoid mention of the murder to anyone involved with the office. Nina had originally spared Charlotte to protect her. But now it seemed like a prudent policy to continue for all sorts of reasons.

Even so, there was no reason for Nina to remain on Charlotte's shitlist. "Charlotte," she said, in her warmest tones, "I just want you to know how much I appreciate all you've done for me. Talking Henry into interviewing me and everything."

"That was no big deal. Henry will interview almost anybody. He's only the first step. If he likes you he'll turn you over to Eddie. And that you earned on your own."

"Doesn't it usually work the other way? Doesn't the aide usually interview you first, and after that you get passed on to the chief?" Nina asked.

"Henry's really more of a figurehead around here. Surely you've caught on to that. Didn't you notice how eccentric he is?"

"He seemed a little fuzzy."

"Fuzzy." Charlotte sniffed. "It's more than that. I could tell you stories. . . ." She drifted off.

"What kind of stories?"

"Oh, basically we spend our working days protecting him."

"From what?"

"For example, you'll never believe what happened last year. Henry was down in Washington, at some mass transit hearings that Congress was conducting. And he . . . oh, hold on for a second." Nina heard muffled voices discussing someone named Daria Gonzalez who was in the waiting room. "You still there?" Charlotte asked Nina when the muffled voices ceased.

"Yeah, I'm here. You were talking about last year when Carr was in D.C."

"Oh, yeah, that was really something. Remind me to tell you about it sometime. But right now, I've really gotta go. My eleven o'clock is here. Talk to you soon. And good luck on Wednesday. Just remember, Margaret doesn't like cute and she doesn't like coy. You'll do fine." And she hung up without ever telling Nina what kind of trouble Henry Carr got into down in Washington.

CHAPTER 24

"Meet me for lunch."

"Nina, I was just going to call you," Ida said.

"No kidding." Nina leaned back in her office chair and put her feet up on her wastepaper basket. It wasn't an especially satisfactory footrest, but it would do. "I thought I'd cut you off at the pass," she told her mother.

"What do you mean?" Although Ida sounded as if she already knew.

"I assume you've spoken to Laura this morning."

"Yeah, and what's this about—"

"Save it."

"Excuse me?"

"I'll meet you for lunch. We'll discuss it then."

"Where should I meet you?" Her mother was champing at the bit to ask a million questions and did not appreciate being reined in. "I have Dr. Weinstein this afternoon." Ida Fischman was in training to break the all-time record for continuous treatment by a psychoanalyst.

"What time?"

"Two-thirty."

"Okay. I'll meet you halfway. How about the Empire Szechuan on Sixty-eighth and Columbus?"

"I make it a practice never to eat Chinese food before sundown," Ida said.

"Like John Cheever and his gin?"

"Exactly." An addiction to Chinese food ran in the Fischman family.

"Okay. Where do you want to go?" Their old meeting place, Bagel Nosh on Seventy-first and Broadway, had closed years ago and they had never found a satisfactory replacement.

"I'm sort of in the mood for matzo ball soup. How about Fine and Schapiro on Seventy-second?"

"Good idea. I'll try to be there by twelve-thirty."

"See you then," her mother said. "And be prepared to tell all."

"You know me. Reticence isn't my long suit."

When she got off the phone, Nina picked up her latest draft of a motion for summary judgment. How long had she been drafting these things, she asked herself, as she idly added a few commas. Too long was the obvious answer. Her motion practice was like aerobics—once she had achieved minimum proficiency, she had stopped improving. Now she was just going through the motions, so to speak. And like aerobics, she was ready to give it up. They had just come out with a study that linked faithful attendance at aerobics class with inner ear damage. She had a feeling that chronic litigation in Housing Court could do far more inner ear damage than jumping up and down a few times a week.

It was time to stop and do something else. She had only said that hundreds of times over the years. But now it looked as if she was actually going to *do* something else. And the thought gave her a stomachache.

It was a nice enough day for a stroll up to Seventy-second

Street, but Nina wasn't getting paid to stroll. She thought about being unemployed in L.A., where she would have all the time in the world. She could go to the gym every day, she thought, and do whatever nonimpact activity she chose. She could even swim, since Nina would have time for shampooing and moisturizing and all those attendant activities that made water sports so time-consuming. But she was too old to be idealistic about the gym. She knew she would never turn herself into a superb physical specimen. It was like motion practice.

On the other hand, the Public Advocate's office might be perfect for her. After all, she was a people person. Or so she had pretended all these years. Was she really a people person? If so, why did she always let her answering machine pick up and why did she often pretend not to see acquaintances in the street? Why did she feel as if she could go for weeks with just Chinese food and a stack of novels and not see anybody?

And what about Jonathan? Could she live without him, or was he up there with the moo shu pork and Anne Tyler?

Maybe she would walk up to Fine and Schapiro after all. If she was going to obsess, she might as well simultaneously burn up a few calories.

She slipped into her spring jacket, a most prized possession that she had hunted down at the Searle outlet in Secaucus. It was one of those swingy three-quarter-length styles in a rich rust color. Rust did not do much for her, but lately she had been wearing it anyway. She had tired of the delicate blues that lit up her eyes and made her skin look pinker. It was probably a sign of age. Looking pretty was no longer necessarily the primary goal.

Fine and Schapiro was an old-fashioned kosher deli, one of the few left in the city which kept up the tradition of semi-nasty male waiters who wore pale blue gray cotton jackets with kishka stains on them. Nina got there before her mother. It used to be that everywhere Nina went, Ida was waiting for her. But lately Nina got there first and it made her think that the power balance was shifting. That Ida, instead of eagerly awaiting the time when her daughter would deign to grant her an audience, was just fitting Nina into her schedule.

It was as if the mother from her childhood, the Ida Fischman who was always tired and never had enough time or money and was worn as thin as the cotton housedresses that comprised her summer wardrobe—well, that Ida Fischman seemed to have disappeared. She had been replaced by someone who knew how to have a good time. Her early years of widowhood had been difficult, but she had adjusted amazingly well, retiring and traveling and subscribing and auditing courses.

This also made Nina wonder, because Ida always claimed that she had loved being married and having small children. But it was undeniable that Ida seemed so much less miserable now that her husband was dead and her children were grown and living away from home.

Ida had blossomed late in life, living alone in the kind of social vacuum that drove other old ladies into a depression. And Nina couldn't help but think that women like her mother and herself did best when they could do whatever they wanted to, whenever they wanted to do it. They weren't natural imperialists, like her sister Laura, who thrived on running her own little empire out in Park Slope. Nina and Ida were isolationists, happy with their Chinese takeout and stacks of paperbacks.

That's what Nina was thinking as she sat in Fine and Schapiro and stared at the counter full of pastramis and corned beefs and tongues. Tongue was something Nina had eaten quite regularly as a small child until one day she had suddenly realized what it was.

Nina was sitting there, quite happily getting herself all worked up about her theory of isolationism, when a small voice piped up. You're full of shit, it said. There *was* that to be considered, Nina agreed. I probably am full of shit, she thought. Her theory was obviously a carefully constructed charade to prevent her from ever moving forward in her life. Resulting, no doubt, from the paralyzing terror that arises from the thought of sharing your life with another human being. Or maybe not.

Ida arrived in a purple tunic and purple pants, topped off by her chunky amethyst beads and earrings. Many older women of Ida's type paid frequent visits to Astro Gallery of Gems on Thirty-fourth Street. And they dropped a fair amount of money there. There was some cachet about unpolished semiprecious stones among the retired schoolteacher crowd that Nina could never quite understand. And amethysts seemed to be their favorite, since they all wore a lot of purple.

"Nice day," her mother said.

"Finally. Soon it will be time to bare our upper arms." Nina had spent so many years worrying about her legs that she had completely missed the fact that her arms were going. Last summer was the first time that she noticed that she was starting to resemble her grandmother in a tank top.

"You can get around to baring your upper arms some other time," Ida said. "Right now it's time to bare your soul. Laura tells me that you're engaged. Is that true? Am I missing something?"

A kishka-stained waiter came by. "Menus?" he asked.

The concept of a menu in a kosher deli was ludicrous. There were pastrami devotees and corned beef devotees and that was that. The only real question was whether you were in the mood for a knish. And if you were, should it be potato or kasha. The Fischman women ordered what they always did—one pastrami sandwich and one potato knish to share with matzo ball soup all around. And a cream soda for Nina and a Cel-Ray for Ida. Nina had never seen a Cel-Ray soda outside of a kosher deli. Did they exist? And why were cream sodas so named, when they had nothing to do with cream? These were kosher deli mysteries that she had never gotten to the bottom of. Even though she had consumed hundreds of cream sodas in her childhood, in delis all over the Bronx, on Westchester and Jerome avenues, on White Plains and Fordham roads.

"Why do they call it a cream soda?" she asked Ida.

"You always ask me that and I never know the answer. Besides, you're being evasive. Answer my question. Are you getting married?" She peered closely at Nina's left hand. "I don't see a ring."

A ring. Nina hadn't even thought about a ring. After all these years, she still had a low Jap Quotient. She launched into an explanation about what had happened the night before and how Danielle had proposed to both of them. "So I don't know how seriously to take it," Nina said. "I can't tell if it's real or not."

"What did Jonathan say after the two of you got home?"

"Nothing."

"And I assume you didn't mention it either?"

"Nope."

"Typical Nina behavior. You obsess to death about every trivial little detail, but when it comes to major life decisions, things just sort of slip your mind."

"Well, I think I might be avoiding the issue."

"How come?" Ida asked. "Don't you want to get married? For a change of pace?"

Nina laughed. "A change of pace. That's about as good a reason as any, I guess."

"Laura also tells me that you're moving to California. Is this true?"

"Jonathan is probably being transferred to L.A. So I thought as long as I was marrying him, I might as well go along with him."

"Sounds reasonable. But none of this seems too definite. To put it mildly."

"Right. Which is why I'm going on a job interview next Wednesday."

"For a job in New York?"

"Yeah. With the Public Advocate's office."

"Henry Carr. Whatever happened with him? Did you make any progress toward finding out who killed Jonathan's doorman?"

"I think I kinda gave up. I wasn't getting anywhere and then I got distracted by all this business about California and the job with Carr's office."

"What about the mailman?"

"What *about* the mailman?"

"Is he still pimping?"

"I guess. We met one of the women who works for him. The one that Carr was following around. She was very nice. Her name was Kristen. She had the greatest African violet collection in her living room. They were all fully in bloom. How do you think she keeps them that way?"

"She probably hides the other ones in her bedroom until they bloom again," Ida said. "And then she brings them back out into the living room."

"I never thought of that. What a good idea."

"Nina, don't you think it's odd?"

"What, hiding your African violets?"

"No, the mailman being a pimp. It's shocking, isn't it? Especially the way everyone ignores it and just lets it go on."

"Ma, this is New York City. People step over dead bodies in the street."

"That what's everyone always says, but it's not true. New Yorkers are natural yentas. They love a scandal. And this is such a perfect one. I would have thought that someone would have exposed both him and Carr by now."

"Exposed them?" Nina asked. "Exposed them how?"

"I don't know. The *Post* would have run a headline. Or 'Hard Copy' would have a confidential videotape of him pimping in the mailroom or the New York City Public Advocate coming to visit Kristen."

"Sol Wachtler got dressed up in disguises and ran all over New York and New Jersey without being exposed."

"But eventually it all came out," Ida said.

"Not until Joy Silverman called her friend at the FBI."

"But eventually it did. And if Joy Silverman hadn't called her friend at the FBI, then somebody else would have called their friend somewhere else. I mean, after it was all out in the open, it turned out that a lot of people knew what was going on. One of them would have contacted the *Post* after a while."

"I guess."

"And this is even juicier. Not only do you have a public official stalking a woman, but she's a hooker. And you have a federal employee pimping on the premises. Even without the dead doorman, it's just too good to keep a lid on."

"So you call the *Post*." Nina turned her attention to her soup, which had just arrived.

"Me? No, I'm not going to call the *Post*. But I bet somebody else will. Or already has."

"What do you mean, already has? Have you read anything in the paper?"

"No."

"So nobody has, right?"

"Maybe."

"What are you getting at?"

"Oh, nothing, Just a few idle thoughts. Never mind." She waved her hand and picked up her spoon. "Don't want my matzo ball to get cold," she said. "Now, am I supposed to give you a bridal shower?"

They both laughed at the idea.

CHAPTER 25

Nina was cheating on Jonathan. Or at least that was how she felt. All week long, while he talked about getting married and moving to California, she kept meaning to mention her interview at the Public Advocate's office. But she never quite got around to it. And here she was, sneaking off to see someone about a job in New York, when she should have been registering at Bloomingdale's and checking out the real estate classifieds in the *Los Angeles Times*. But this job would probably come to nothing, the way that every other job over the years had. And then there would be no damage done.

Margaret Connell had Prudence send Nina in right away. Charlotte had said that Connell was a no-bullshit type, and she certainly seemed forthcoming. She didn't bother with a handshake, but waved Nina in with a hand that held a lit cigarette. "Sorry," she said, gesturing with the cigarette. "It's a miserable habit, but since it's my office, you get to put up with it. Unless you're allergic or something."

"I'm not allergic to anything." The Polish peasant stock that had given Nina her low center of gravity had paid off when it came to her immune system.

"Well, sit down." Margaret Connell leaned across her desk and pulled a stack of redwells off a chair. She looked around for a place to put them and finally stacked them over in a corner, on the floor. "Do I have your résumé?" She rummaged around the papers on her desk.

"I don't know. Do you?"

"I'm sure I do, but I can't seem to find it. Do you happen to have an extra copy?"

"Not on me. Sorry." Maybe Nina wasn't the kind of person who was allergic to things, but neither was she the kind of person who remembered to take an extra copy of her résumé.

"I don't have your résumé and you don't have your résumé. So where do we go from here?"

"Wherever you want. As you said, it's your office."

"Right." Connell gave a phlegmy croak that was meant to serve as a laugh. "Well, Eddie says he wants to hire you. Unless I absolutely hate you. Is there any reason why I should absolutely hate you?"

"I don't think so. Nobody absolutely hates me. I'm not the type. Sometimes I wish I were."

"Do you also wish you had allergies?" Boy, Margaret Connell had her number. And it hadn't taken long.

"Not really."

"There's nothing romantic about allergies, you know."

"I know." Nina nodded her agreement.

"*I* don't think so, anyway. I've never liked those consumptive Camille types. Although the boss man does."

"Mr. Carr?"

"Yeah, Henry would have made a good Victorian."

"He seemed to have quite a few fond memories of his childhood."

Margaret laughed again. This time her croak was more of a bark. "That's one way to put it. Old Henry really lives in the past. He's a little fuzzy. Sometimes he reminds me of the guy in *Arsenic and Old Lace*. The one who thought he was Teddy Roosevelt. You know the one I mean?''

"Of course. That took place in Brooklyn Heights, his neighborhood. Didn't it?''

"Right.'' Connell stabbed out her cigarette and leaned across her desk. "When that movie with Woody Harrelson and Wesley Snipes came out, I saw someone wearing a T-shirt that said 'White Men Can't Think.' It reminded me of Henry.''

Nina didn't know if this was some kind of a trap. Why would an employee bad-mouth her boss that way? On the other hand, why wouldn't she? Most of Nina's working life had been spent in rooms with other female colleagues making fun of slightly dim male bosses. There was no reason to think that this place was any different. She was soon to find out, since Charlotte Klein picked that moment to pop her head in.

"Well, hello there.'' Charlotte came over and gave Nina a kiss on the cheek. "Meeting some of the inmates?''

"Only me,'' Margaret said. "We were talking about Henry. I was just about to launch into my 'White Men Can't Think' monologue.''

Charlotte giggled conspiratorially. She looked good, Nina thought. Just as dumpling-like as ever, but somehow more juicy and delectable. Charlotte bobbed her curly head up and down. "Yeah, Henry's some piece of work.''

"Well,'' said Nina, "I must say that's not much of a recommendation for working here.''

Connell waved her hand dismissively. "Oh, don't worry about *him*. *We* run the office.''

"The two of you?''

"Eddie, me, Charlotte. A few others. Maybe you.'' She

gave Nina a crooked smile. "Does that bother you? That our boss is completely ineffectual and a little cracked?"

"Well, it makes me wonder about his job stability. Because I assume that if he goes, we go." It was something that hadn't occurred to Nina before. If she did solve Ray's murder and Henry Carr was implicated, it would probably mean that New York City would be getting a new Public Advocate. And Nina would be headed back to Legal Services.

"Ah, Henry's weathered scandals before."

"Like what?"

Margaret Connell ran her hand through her hair. It was the color that red hair gets just before it goes gray, all drab, an untamed and bushy mess. Somewhere above her right temple was a lone bobby pin, attempting to control the cascades of red-gray waves. But it was merely a finger in the dike, since Connell's hair had a mind of its own. Nina couldn't tell exactly how old she was, but she'd say Connell was definitely pre-baby boom, probably born sometime during the war. She was bone-thin in an unselfconscious way, wearing baggy clothes and sitting with her legs slightly apart. Not the kind of thin that comes from dieting, the Helen Gurley Brown, Nancy Reagan macrocephalic kind of thin, but the kind of thin that used to be called skinny, back when people didn't say it with awe and envy. Reading glasses with bright red frames perched on the bridge of her nose.

Connell sighed and lit another cigarette. "The first scandal that Henry weathered was when he was in the City Council."

"Margaret and Henry go way back," Charlotte said. "Was that the one with the prostitute in Chinatown?"

"That's right," Margaret said. "The next time he almost went down was when he was deputy mayor. And guess what?"

"Another hooker?" Nina asked.

"You got it."

"I'd say he had a bit of a problem."

"Poor Henry." Connell ran her hand through her hair again.

"He had been abstaining for a while, hadn't he?" Charlotte asked Margaret.

"Yeah, he was in remission with this whore thing for a while. But lately it's gotten worse."

Nina wondered whether Margaret would have been so forthcoming if Charlotte hadn't been in the room. Nina was lucky, they had a nice girl thing going among the three of them and Nina was not about to question it. Besides, "Why are you telling me all this?" wasn't the kind of thing that Nina would ever say to anyone under any circumstances. Nina's favorite line was "Tell me more." In this case it didn't seem to be necessary.

"He seems really obsessed with this last one," Connell said to Charlotte. "I've told you about her, haven't I?"

"You mean the one who dumped him?" Charlotte asked.

"Yeah, that one." She turned to Nina. "You see, this prostitute he claims to be in love with spurned him and now he's following her all over the place."

"He told you this?"

"I heard it straight from the horse's mouth, when the horse got drunk at one of our poker parties. We were sharing a cab home to Brooklyn."

"Oh, do you live in Brooklyn too?" Nina asked.

"Where else would someone like me live?"

"Inwood."

Connell thought about it for a minute. "Good answer," she finally said. "Eddie was right. I don't absolutely hate you. In fact, I think I like you."

"Thank you. I like you too." Nina pushed her hand through her own mop.

"I told you you'd like her," Charlotte said.

"So you were sharing a cab back to Brooklyn . . ." Nina prompted.

"Right. We were headed down Second Avenue somewhere in the Thirties when Henry starts banging on the bulletproof partition and makes the driver stop the cab. Then he goes running down some side street and finally comes back, drenched with sweat and looking disappointed. He gets back in the cab and says, 'It wasn't her.' So I asked him who 'her' was and he tells me this long ridiculous story about some hooker that he claims to be in love with."

Nina had a choice. She could sit here primly with her legs crossed at the ankles and her lips pursed into a small **O** and just nod encouragingly. Or she could plunge ahead. She uncrossed her ankles. There was something about Margaret Connell that made you want to plunge. Besides, with Charlotte there, egging Margaret on, there was a good chance that Nina could find out some interesting stuff about Kristen.

"I've met her," Nina said.

"Who?"

"Her. The 'her' that Carr was talking about. Henry's hooker. I've met her."

Connell narrowed her eyes and gave Nina a look that was a search and destroy mission unto itself. "Are you from DOI?" she asked.

"I don't even know what DOI stands for."

"Department of Investigation." Connell's eyes shifted to the ceiling and she thumped the side of her head with the palm of her hand. "Of course. How stupid of me. You're a reporter. Did Artie send you?"

"Who's Artie?"

"Never mind Artie. Who is she?" she asked Charlotte. Not waiting for an answer, she turned back to Nina. "Who are you?"

"I'm not an investigator *or* a reporter. I'm just sort of an amateur . . . yenta, I guess you'd say."

"Now, Nina," Charlotte said, "don't undersell yourself." She turned to Margaret. "Nina is a yenta *extraordinaire*."

Nina crossed her legs and demurely folded her hands in her lap. "Thank you," she said.

"But I don't get it," Charlotte said. "Is this a coincidence? Or did you have something else on your mind when you faxed me your résumé?"

"Well . . ." Nina considered how pissed Charlotte might be about being mercilessly manipulated. But Nina was in too deep now to pretend that it was all a coincidence. And she doubted whether Charlotte and Margaret would buy anything except the truth. Besides, she had a strong suspicion that Charlotte's response could go one way or the other, depending on Nina's presentation. With skillful craftsmanship, Nina could pull her into a conspiratorial mode, especially when it came to a male boss who she clearly thought was an idiot.

"Well," Nina repeated, "I had always meant to give you a call about the possibility of my working here. But I never actually got around to it until I . . . um . . ."

"Developed another agenda?"

"Yeah, right. But I didn't want you to have to cover for me, so I never mentioned any of this, mostly to protect you."

"I know I'm supposed to appreciate this," Charlotte said, "but I think that I would rather have known what was really going on."

"One always would, wouldn't one?" Margaret said.

"True." Nina nodded, then launched into the whole story

of Ray's murder and Mundo the pimp and Kristen the hooker. Charlotte and Margaret sat there and listened, clearly taking in every word. Nina had just about gotten up to the part about Kristen's African violets, when Charlotte suddenly looked at her watch.

"Shit," Charlotte said. "I'm gonna be late if I don't leave this absolute minute."

"Late for what?"

"Acupuncture."

"I thought you were looking awfully good," Nina said. "Is that your secret?"

"Yeah, it's all in the herbs. But I want to hear the end of this."

"Well, she can't stop now," Margaret said. "And leave me hanging."

"Okay, take notes. And, Nina?"

"Yeah?"

"I forgive you. Even though you haven't had the good grace to beg for my forgiveness."

"Thank you."

"You're welcome." And she was off. There was definitely a swivel to her rounded hips that had never been there before. Nina made a mental note to consider visiting an herbalist.

Meanwhile, Margaret crossed her bony legs, narrowed her eyes and lit another cigarette. "Go on," she told Nina.

"Okay." And she did, with Margaret's rapt attention.

"Poor Henry," Margaret said, when Nina had brought the story up to date. "He had giving whoring up entirely. He had to, you see, when Betty cut back on his allowance. Never underestimate the power of the purse strings."

"I never do. But why does she stay married to him?"

"Inertia. The same reason most of us do what we do. Besides, she's a bit of a drunk. It's sometimes hard for boozers to galvanize into action. Anyway, Henry had been abstaining totally when he met this mailman pimp. What did you say his name was?"

"Mundo," Nina said. "How did someone like Henry Carr meet someone like Mundo? Do you have any idea?"

"Henry had dropped the whores, but he hadn't dropped his whoring friends. You know, it's just like those guys who've given up drinking. They can't help but hang out in their old haunts. At first they stand at the bar and drink ginger ale. But before long they're back on the hard stuff."

"I don't see the analogy," Nina said. "It's not as if Carr spent his evening in bordellos, is it? Isn't that a little old-fashioned?"

"Yeah, I gather that's not the way it works. But there is the occasional party and one of Henry's friends took him someplace one night where he met Kristen. And he was resisting it, but then Mundo moved in and gave him the hard sell. At least that's what Henry told me."

"And he relented?"

"Yeah, he caved."

"Why would Mundo bother? I don't think of pimps as being heavy on marketing."

"Everyone is always trying to sell Henry something," Connell said. "From hookers to vacuum cleaners. Because he's a born sucker. That's why it was such a scream when he was elected Public Advocate."

"Maybe it was more than that," Nina said. "Maybe Mundo knew that Henry was a politician and that he would make a good target for blackmail. And he set that whole thing up and then put the squeeze on him."

"I doubt it. Pimps can't indulge in blackmail. How long do you think they'd last in business if it became known that they blackmailed their clients?"

"I guess you're right."

"Besides, let's say some pimp comes along and tells one of his patrons that if he wants to keep his name out of the papers, he'd better pay up. And he doesn't pay. The pimp can't call his bluff. He can't very well go marching off to the *New York Post* without telling them all about his illegal operation. Which is out of the question, of course."

"You're good at this," Nina said.

"Thank you," Connell said.

"I just wish I could figure out what was going on."

Connell sighed and leaned back in her chair and crossed her legs. She was wearing some sort of jumper-like garment that came down to the middle of her calf. If I had legs like that, Nina thought, I'd wear one of those little spandex skirts that looks like an Ace bandage.

"Look," said Margaret, "I'm going to do something that is probably against my better judgment. After all, I just met you. And I don't always like sticking my nose into places where I could get stung. But you *are* a friend of Charlotte's. Even though apparently you used her."

"I was protecting her," Nina insisted.

"Yeah, yeah. Well, forget about Charlotte. The truth is that my curiosity has got the best of me. Funny, I don't give in to much. Men, politics, booze, I can hold them all off. Cigarettes and my curiosity, those are the only things that really bring me to my knees."

"I know what you mean. Just substitute Chinese food for cigarettes for me."

"Anyway, I guess we're going to have to call Artie after all," Margaret said.

"Yeah, let's call Artie."

"Might as well." She reached for her Rolodex, which looked as if it had been around since the inception of city government.

"Who's Artie?"

"A reporter."

"Oh, speaking of the *New York Post* . . ."

"He's not from the *Post*. He's from *Newsday*."

"The classy tabloid," Nina said. "*Times* Lite."

"You can't beat their local coverage."

"Why are we calling Artie?"

"Because he called me. About a month ago. It was a very strange phone call. And I can't help but think that it had something to do with this."

"What did he call you about?" Nina asked.

"Henry. He wanted to know how mentally balanced he was. Whether he had any history of extra-marital affairs. The interesting thing, now that I think of it, is that Artie is the one who covered the Wachtler mess for *Newsday*. Maybe he thought Henry could be the new Sol Wachtler."

"I think he could, don't you? If what Kristen told me was true, with the disguises and all. Did Artie ever end up writing anything about Henry?"

"No."

"Are you sure?" Nina asked.

"Believe me, if he did I would have heard about it. But it gives me an idea as to a theory about how your doorman got murdered."

"What's that?"

"Well, according to you, this doorman was being very co-operative, letting Henry in the building and all. He must have had a motive."

"Maybe Henry was paying him off," Nina said.

"Maybe. But here's what I think. The doorman was facilitating Henry's stalking, but meanwhile he was planning on double-crossing him and selling the story to the tabloids. And his contact was Artie, which makes sense since he's still thought of as the reporter who covered Wachtler."

Nina broke in. "And Henry got wind of it. And had Ray killed before he could spill his guts to the tabloids."

"There's only one problem with that theory," Margaret said. "Henry's always the last to know everything. He never gets wind of anything."

"Well, maybe Henry's wife found out. And didn't want her husband involved in a scandal," Nina said, trotting out one of her old theories. "Or what about Eddie Kornbluth? He's pinned his whole career on Henry Carr. Eddie's got a lot to lose if Henry goes down."

"So do I. Who else is going to hire a chain-smoker in this day and age?"

"So are we going to call Artie?"

"Let's." Margaret checked a ragged card in her Rolodex and punched in a number. "Artie Feingold, please." She waited awhile. "Artie Feingold, please," she said again. Then she cut off whoever was on the other end. "Listen, I've got something for him from the mayor's office. He's waiting for it. And I've got to run out of here in about thirty seconds. So it's now or never." Only about fifteen seconds went by before she smiled, raised her eyebrows triumphantly and said "Hiya, Artie, how ya' doin'? It's Maggie Connell."

Nina was impressed. Maybe no one wanted to hire a chain-smoker in this day and age, but she had a feeling they'd make an exception for Margaret Connell.

"Fine, fine. Henry's fine. Everything here is just hunkydory . . . Yeah, we're advocating like hell for the public. As always. Listen, remember that last chat we had? About Henry's mental health? . . . Yeah, right . . . Anyway, I have this theory that I want to test out on you. You just have to answer yes or no. You don't have to tell me anything that I haven't already figured out. Fair enough? . . . Good. I think this is what happened. Tell me if I'm right. Somebody called you with a story about Henry, for which

he expected some financial remuneration, is that right? . . .
Okay, the story had something to do with a lady of the evening, is that right? . . . And you thought that maybe you
had another Sol Wachtler saga on your hands . . . Right
. . . But then before you had a chance to make the arrangement, the guy stopped calling you and you had no way to
reach him. . . . Not even a code name, huh? Well, did he
sound like a Hispanic guy? . . . He did, huh? . . . Yeah,
well I can't give you any more information right now.
Maybe later. Listen, Artie? You print any word of this and I
kill you, understood? Or at the very least of it, you'll never
hear the second half . . . Okay, you'll be the first. Bye."

"Very impressive," Nina said.

"Yeah, well that's the kind of stuff you have to do around
this place if you come work here. Think you're up for it,
Nina Fischman?"

"I'd be in your shadow." Nina hated to sound pandering,
but she meant it.

"So now we know why Ray was killed." Margaret looked
like she was thoroughly enjoying herself.

"Amazing. You accomplished in one phone call what I
couldn't do by running all over town."

"But what we still don't know," Margaret said, "is who
did it."

"Right." Nina waited expectantly.

"Well, I found out why. It's up to you to find out who."

"Oh."

"You should eliminate Henry, Betty and Eddie. I know
them all intimately and I know that none of them did it."

"How can you be sure?"

"Because they all have the biggest mouths in the world,"
Margaret said. "And even if they didn't spill their guts to
me, I would have noticed something."

"I believe you. So where does that leave us?"

"Well, whichever way this comes out, it probably leaves me unemployed. Since as soon as this murder is solved, it's sure to hit the papers. And that's sure to be the end of Henry's job."

"You think he'll resign?"

"After a stalking story runs in *Newsday*? I'd say so. He'd have to."

"And you wouldn't be able to stay on?"

Margaret turned and looked out of the window. "Nah. Whoever replaces Henry will have his own coterie of aging boy nerds and gravel-voiced old-maid chain-smokers to bring here. And we'll be gently shown the door."

"So why did you call Artie? Why not just leave well enough alone?"

Margaret turned back to Nina. She shrugged. "I don't know. I felt like it."

Nina knew what she meant.

CHAPTER 26

That evening, as Nina got off the subway, she couldn't stop thinking about Margaret Connell. How she had plunged ahead and called Artie even if it ultimately meant her job. It was brave, and shortsighted in a way that Nina admired. If Nina had been in Connell's situation, would she have made the call? Ultimately, perhaps, but first she would have spent a couple of hours obsessing about it.

As she walked up Broadway, her mind roamed over various dinner options. Now that the specter of cohabitation and, even more terrifying, marriage loomed on the horizon, she cherished the thought of an evening alone. Eating whatever, wearing whatever, having total control of the television.

She knew what she wanted for dinner. It was something she ate as a child, which no one ever ate anymore. Her generation had spurned it for more sophisticated culinary ventures. But every now and then, when she was alone, Nina would roll back the clock and pretend she was back in the Bronx, pick up the phone and order shrimp and lobster sauce. And an egg roll. With extra duck sauce. She never had the nerve to order it in a restaurant. But at home, only her deliveryman knew for sure.

As she entered her building, she stopped to pick up a flyer from a nearby Chinese restaurant. Chinese take-out menus had become loathsome objects, up there with pigeons and rats, considered a vile plague and banned from many buildings. Only old ladies who kept everything, and a few eccentrics like Nina, appreciated their presence. She collected them like stamps, keeping them in a manila folder and leafing through them when an evening like this presented itself. It was silly, she knew, since they were all pretty much the same. But she found it an enjoyable ritual nevertheless.

The menu in the lobby was from a yet untested establishment named Cottage Jewel. It was nearby on Broadway and the shrimp and lobster sauce was a pricey $9.95. Why did so many Chinese restaurants have cottage or jewel in their names? There was probably a historical significance to those things that had become completely mundane—who was General Tseng, for example, and why was chicken with water chestnuts named after him? These were the thoughts that occupied Nina's mind as she opened her mailbox.

It was Wednesday and *The New Yorker* had finally arrived, along with several catalogs. Why any major retailing chain would think that Nina would order pants by mail, she couldn't imagine. Nevertheless, such catalogs continued to fill her box. Today her mail was all squashed in, crumpling a postcard with a picture of Cuernavaca on it. Everyone seemed to be going to Mexico this year. It had become prohibitively expensive to go to Amsterdam to sleep in Dam Square, the way they used to.

Nina looked mournfully at the crumpled postcard. She wished she had a nice mailroom like Jonathan did. And a mailman who would put a rubber band around her magazines and catalogs if they couldn't fit into her box. And then put the neat little parcel on a nice Bombay Company mahogany reproduction table like the one in Jonathan's mailroom. A mailman like Mundo.

Ha, Nina thought. What would happen to him if *Newsday* ran a story about Henry Carr's stalking? That might be the end of Mundo's pimping empire. Which was something she hadn't previously considered.

By the time Nina had entered her living room, she was already dialing her mother's number. Ida's answering machine clicked in. Oh shit, Nina thought, where is she? But in the middle of Nina's message, Ida picked up.

"I'm here," her mother said.

"Don't you answer your phone?"

"Well, I was watering my plants."

"You're supposed to be a needy old lady who's just dying for human contact. What are you doing screening your calls?"

"I'm entitled." That had been the theme of Ida Fischman's several decades of psychotherapy. Her entitlements and lack thereof.

"Okay, okay. You're entitled. Why don't you write a self-help book already? You could call it *I'm Entitled, You're Entitled.*"

"Is that why you called?"

"Listen, remember the conversation we had last week in Fine and Schapiro?"

"Yes."

"What were you saying about Jonathan's mailman? I guess I wasn't listening."

"You weren't."

"I know, I know. You're entitled to be listened to. I apologize."

"That's okay. You're my daughter. Listening to me is optional for you."

"Thank you."

"Anyway, I was saying that I thought it was only a matter of time until someone exposed him. It's such a good scandal, running a pimping operation out of an Upper East Side mailroom."

"Exactly. You know," Nina said, "I've been so focused on what Henry Carr had to lose by being exposed, I just didn't think what would happen to Mundo. I mean, Henry Carr has put a lifetime into his career, but Mundo probably has also."

"I'd say so."

"You know, Ma, there are some interesting parallels between the two of them. Henry's got his wife and Mundo's got his hookers. Neither has to live on their government salary."

"True."

"Well, let me run something by you. There's this *Newsday* reporter who says that someone, probably Ray the doorman, called him."

"When did he call? Before or after Ray died?"

"Let's say before."

"Well, we couldn't very well say after, could we?"

"No, we couldn't. Anyway, this reporter says that he got this phone call about Henry Carr and his stalking. That he was stalking a prostitute. And this hypothetical Ray wanted money for the story. But before the reporter could firm up the deal, Ray had disappeared. And the reporter, who didn't even know his name, had no way to reach him. Do you think it could have been Mundo who got rid of Ray?"

"Absolutely," Ida said. "You see, I think that the Mundo part of the story makes an even better headline than the Henry Carr part."

"You do? You don't think that a high-level public official turning out to be a stalker is news?"

"It's been done."

"Wait a minute. The Wachtler story didn't have the hooker angle," Nina said.

"Okay, Carr is still a good story. But I think that it would definitely be in Mundo's interest to see that the story didn't run. Also, you're overlooking one thing."

"What's that?"

"You've met Mundo, haven't you?"

"Yup."

"And what did you think?" Ida asked.

"He gave me the creeps."

"Do you think he's capable of murder?"

"Absolutely."

"Well, don't you think that counts?"

"With my instincts, I'm not sure."

Ida chose to ignore Nina's self-deprecation. It was something she had been trained to do in psychotherapy. "So how did you find out about the reporter?"

"Someone on Henry Carr's staff told me. You know, I had an interview over there today."

"Oh, right. So do you have a new job? In addition to getting married and moving to California?"

"Well, it's moot now. Once the murder's solved and the press gets hold of Henry the stalker, that's the end of him. He won't be in a position to hire me or anyone else."

"So you won't have to deal with that conflict," Ida said.

"Right. Now if only Jonathan would decide to stay in New York, I wouldn't have to deal with anything. Things could stay just the way they are."

"Nina, I thought you were sick of things the way they are."

"I am. But that doesn't necessarily mean I want them to change."

"I see. I think."

"Listen, I'll talk to you later, okay?" Nina said, and hung up. She glanced at the take-out menu but put it down. The shrimp and lobster sauce would have to wait.

Nina dialed Jonathan's number but got his machine. Then she went through all her coat pockets until she scraped together ten dollars. Sometimes you just had to take a cab.

Finding a cab in Manhattan had been easy for years. There were hordes of desperate immigrants from Pakistan and Haiti and Eastern Europe, driving around most of the day in empty taxis. It made life easier for a certain kind of person, but made for a more aggressive kind of driving. All you had to do was step off the curb and raise a finger a mere few inches and some crazed driver would cut across five lanes of traffic to your side. There were still people in New York who complained about not being able to get a cab. But these were not people who, in Nina's opinion, had any idea of what was going on.

Nina got a driver who seemed to understand where Eighty-second and Third was, but had an uncertain foot on the gas pedal. He'd speed and brake alternately and Nina considered getting out. She knew she never would, of course, for the same reason she never bothered to return a container of cottage cheese that had gone bad.

"Which side?" he asked, as they drove up Third Avenue. He was Asian, maybe from Korea or China. Certainly not Japanese, judging from his monosyllabic name.

"Right. The right side," Nina said. He immediately pulled over to the left and stopped the cab. "Thank you," Nina said, and tipped him well. What else was she going to do?

The evening doorman recognized her and let her in. "Is Jonathan home yet?" she asked him.

"I haven't seen him."
"Well, I have the key. I'll go on up. Okay?"
"Sure."
But when she got into the elevator, she pushed 26.

CHAPTER 27

Kristen was home and on the phone. She looked alarmed when she opened the door and saw Nina standing there. But she motioned her in and pointed her to the couch. "Listen, Mom," Kristen said into the phone, "I've gotta go. I'll see you at the wake . . . Yeah, seven o'clock. Okay, bye."

"A wake?" Nina asked, getting a running start on intrusiveness.

"A death in the family," Kristen explained.

"Oh." Did that mean she wasn't Norwegian? Scandinavians were mostly Lutheran, Nina thought. They didn't have wakes. But maybe Kristen was half Norwegian and half Irish. And the death had been on the Irish side. Or maybe a Protestant aunt had married a Catholic husband who had died. Why did Nina care? Why couldn't she stop thinking about it? Maybe it was some kind of biochemical imbalance.

Kristen walked over to the windowsill and started fussing with her plants.

"You've got such beautiful African violets," Nina said. "How do you keep them in bloom?"

"I feed them special food. And then I just throw them out when they stop blooming."

"You do?" It made Nina's blood run cold.

"Yeah. It's actually cheaper than buying cut flowers."

"I guess." Cut flowers were another thing that Nina had trouble with. If something couldn't be consumed or recycled, she stayed away. She never remembered anyone having cut flowers back in the Bronx, except for an occasional birthday corsage and a centerpiece taken home from a Bar Mitzvah. In fact, she was pretty sure that there hadn't even been a florist in her old neighborhood.

"Is that what you came here to ask me? I don't think so."

"No, I'm not really that interested in house plants. I used to have a lot of them, years ago when I had nothing better to do than cut classes and smoke marijuana. But eventually the plants started competing for my time and attention with the gym and *The New Yorker* and washing my panty hose. The panty hose won."

"So why are you here?" Kristen asked.

"I . . . um . . . wanted to correct a wrong impression that I think I left you with the last time we spoke."

"What was that?"

"Well, at the time I thought that Ray the doorman had been blackmailing Henry Carr. As it turns out, I was wrong. But not that wrong. Actually, he was planning on selling the whole story to *Newsday*. Somebody stopped him. And I have a strong feeling that it was your boss."

"My boss?"

"I'm not talking about your uncle Henry the optometrist."

"You mean Mundo?"

"I do. Kristen, I've been thinking a lot about something you said."

"What's that?" Kristen had sat down in the chintz-covered chair. Her legs were crossed and she was nervously swinging one leg. Her hands gripped the padded arms and her jaw was clenched in a tight malocclusion. She did not look relaxed.

"You told me that you didn't think that Ray was black-mailing Henry. You said, and I believe I'm quoting you word for word, 'He was interested in money, but I think he planned to take another route.' "

"Well, I guess I was right." Kristen shrugged.

"How did you find out about it?" Nina asked.

Kristen's malocclusion shifted. She dug her fingernails into her palms. Finally, she said, "He was going to cut me in if I cooperated."

"Cooperated in what way?"

"Talked to the reporter. Gave him all the dirt. Told him all about Henry and his disguises. And Mundo and his whole business operation."

"So did you agree to cooperate?"

Kristen uncrossed her legs, got up and walked back over to the window. She looked up and down Third Avenue. "At first I did. When he told me that he could get a hundred thousand dollars and that he would split it down the middle with me. I figured that fifty grand would offer me a way out of all this." She gestured toward her bedroom.

"So what happened?"

"It turned out that Ray was bullshitting me. I should have known. He finally admitted that the reporter hadn't really offered him any money."

"So you told him that all bets were off?"

"Not exactly."

"What do you mean?"

"I never got a chance to."

"Why not?"

"Something happened."

"What happened?"

"Ray went and got himself killed."

"And how did he do that?"

Kristen crossed the room and sat back down in the chair. "Okay, this is what happened. I guess I should have told someone before, but if you were me, you wouldn't have either."

"Maybe you're right," Nina said. "But we won't know until you tell me the rest of your story."

"Can't you guess?"

"I can guess. But go ahead."

"Okay. Well, I got scared. I thought that maybe it wasn't such a good idea that Ray talk to a reporter. That it might ruin everything for me. That I might end up doing jail time."

"But you weren't worried before, when you thought that Ray was going to split a hundred grand with you."

"No, not as worried."

Nina involuntarily raised her eyebrows.

"Look," Kristen snapped, "I'm only human. I'm greedy. I'll admit it."

"So what did you do when you decided that you were scared?"

"I told Mundo."

"Everything?"

"Not that I had originally agreed to cooperate with Ray. Just that Ray was going to talk to a reporter about the pimping and the stalking."

"And what did he say?"

"Mundo is very cool. But I could tell that he was really furious. He cursed a little under his breath and told me to avoid Ray for a while. I said I would."

"And then?"

"Ray was killed."

"How much later?"

"Two days."

"And you didn't tell anyone?"

"No one."

"How could you not?" asked Nina.

"In my business, you get used to not telling people things."

"What about us? When we came asking about blackmail. Did you even think about letting us in on what had gone on?"

"Look, I felt that the tighter I kept my mouth shut the better. I didn't consider myself an accessory to a crime or anything. And I figured the more I talked, the more I would find out. And then the more I would have to conceal."

So that was what had happened. It had to have been Mundo. Funny, Nina thought. She had finally figured out why Ray was killed and who killed him, but extraneous thoughts kept cramming her mind. Like whether Kristen was a Lutheran or a Catholic. "Can I ask you a few more questions?" she finally said, giving in to herself.

"Depends."

"How do you spell your name? With an E-N or I-N at the end?"

"However you like."

"What do you mean?"

Kristen laughed. "It's not really my name, so it's not really spelled more one way than another. I made it up. I thought it was a good name for someone in my profession."

"What's your real name?"

"Valeria. Valeria Constanza DiNardo."

"Valeria. It's pretty. You should have kept it."

"As an adult I can appreciate it. But when I was a kid, everyone in the neighborhood called me malaria."

"So you're Italian?"

"What did you think?"

"I don't know. Norwegian. Or maybe Irish."

"Oh, please. I'm Italian on both sides. My real hair color is darker than yours."

"It looks so natural." So much for Nina's sixth sense about people.

"Yeah, well, my monthly hair care costs would make you cringe. And I don't get to write any of it off, even though it really is a business expense."

"Well, you can't complain. You make enough off the books to compensate," Nina said. "Which reminds me of something else I've been wondering about. Maybe you know the answer."

"What's that?"

"Mundo. He probably does pretty well in the building, doesn't he?"

"Oh, yeah."

"So why does he continue to schlepp mail around? Does he really need such direct personal contact to keep his business going?"

Kristen thought about it for a minute. "No," she said. "He could probably do it by phone, now that he's got it off the ground. I bet he keeps his job for the same reason I schlepp out to Jersey twice a week. He needs the health insurance."

Health insurance. Suddenly Nina felt very vulnerable. All this time, she had been picturing sitting around Los Angeles, swimming and saunaing and reading novels and eating exotic produce. But she hadn't pictured doing all those things while uninsured. She supposed that under COBRA, she could continue her present coverage, but it would cost a fortune. She'd have to get herself on Jonathan's policy, which meant actually going through with a wedding.

It seemed that every question had the same answer. Why don't you quit your job? Why did you get married? Why don't we all run off to the caves on the southern coast of

Crete? Or string puka shells on Maui? Everyone needed the health insurance.

"So what do you do now?" Kristen asked.

"Indeed. What do I do now?" Nina didn't know. Get married. Move. Go to the police. Not necessarily in that order.

CHAPTER 28

The first thing Nina did was to go see if Jonathan was home. All three activities—getting married, moving to California and going to the police—would probably involve him. Before she even opened the door, she heard the "MacNeil-Lehrer Newshour" emanating from the apartment. She considered retreating back to the West Side for shrimp with lobster sauce and an uninterrupted session of "Jeopardy!" But this week was the Teen Tournament of Champions, which was never any fun. Because even if you got everything right, what did it prove? That you were the smartest teenager in America? Besides, running away crosstown wouldn't ultimately solve anything. She was in too deep now.

Nina entered smiling. "Hello there."

"Hi." He sat up on the couch.

"Have I got some news for you," she said.

"And I have some for you."

"You first."

"No, you first."

"No, you."

"Okay," Jonathan said.

Nina knew that the man always had to go first because if

the woman went first then the man would be too distracted to listen, waiting for his turn. And the woman might as well be talking to herself.

"You can forget about Los Angeles," he said.

Was he breaking up with her? Nina didn't think so. He didn't have the right tone, that tension tinged with guilt that she knew all too well. He sounded purely mournful.

"What happened?" she asked, sitting down next to him.

"The agency lost the client. After all that. What a sick business I'm in."

"So that means you get to stay in New York." Nina's heart soared.

"That means my job is hanging by a thread. Whenever a big client walks, heads tend to roll. And mine might be rolling down the hallway any day now."

"You'll find another job." She squeezed his knee. "You always do."

"Yeah, but look how long it took me the last time."

"Don't worry. I'll move in with you. That way, you won't have to worry about the rent." The words had come out before she knew what was happening.

"But I thought that this building offended your sensibilities."

"Sensibilities are for young people," Nina said. She understood it now. She could only let her sensibilities lead her around by the nose for so long. At some point, she and her sensibilities were going to have to part company. Otherwise, it would be just her and her sensibilities living together in a perfect little vacuum. She knew that the time to act was now. Or never. And never would suck her right into that perfect little vacuum.

"I had hoped," she went on, "that everything would be just right. That we would have lots of money and find the perfect place to live, with lots of room and lots of charm. But

I'll tell you something. After the thought of moving to Los Angeles, Third Avenue is looking better and better."

"Well, if that's as romantic as you get, I guess I'll have to take it."

So they weren't Fonda and Redford in *Barefoot in the Park*. Who was? Not even Fonda and Redford. "There's one thing I do want to ask of you," she said.

"What's that?"

"Can we not get married on May twelfth? Can we just do one thing at a time?"

"What's the matter? Holding out for a diamond ring?"

"Yeah. A big one. Emerald cut, if you please." Sometimes Nina felt uneasy about the fact that she and Jonathan joked their way through everything. She supposed that marriage was no joking matter. But if that was the case, then she didn't want any part of it.

"When do you want to move in?"

"How about May twelfth? I have a sudden cancellation for that day."

"Fine. My calendar's clear too." He smoothed her hair back. "So what was your news?" he asked.

"News?"

"Yeah, when you walked in you said you had some news."

"Oh, right." Nina had been so blinded with relief at not having to get married and move to California, that she had totally forgotten about everything else. "Guess who killed Ray?" she said.

"I give up."

"Mundo."

"Mundo, huh? I'll buy it. What made you decide it was him?"

"I talked to a couple of people and got suspicious. So I

went upstairs and paid a visit to Kristen, who confirmed it. She's Italian, by the way."

"Yeah," Jonathan said, "I thought she might be."

"You did?"

"Uh huh. I could tell by the way she talked. She has a real *Saturday Night Fever* accent."

"But that's such a superficial analysis," Nina said. "Based on one movie, you think you know everything about Brooklyn. That accent is socioeconomic. It cuts across ethnic lines. And if you understood more about the boroughs, you'd see that you can't make such oversimplified judgments."

"Was I right or wrong about her? Is she Italian or not?"

"You were right."

"So I *can* make oversimplified judgments."

She had painted herself into a corner. Better change the subject. "Anyway, getting back to Mundo. What should I do? Go to the police?"

"Of course."

"What do you think they'll do?"

"Investigate. They'll talk to Kristen, maybe see if there are any fingerprints in my car that match Mundo's."

"Yeah, they must have his already, since he works for the Post Office. Have they searched your car for prints?"

"I don't know. They still have the car, you know."

"Really? I didn't know. How come it's still impounded? Didn't you try to get it back?"

"What was the point?" he said. "We weren't going out of town and I had nobody to move it for alternate side of the street parking. So I let the cops keep it. I figure it's like having it garaged for free."

She hadn't given Jonathan's car a second thought. All this time she'd had no idea whether it was on the street or in a garage or with the Police Department. Did moving in with

Jonathan mean that she'd have to worry about the car being illegally parked? What other encumbrances lay in wait for her?

"So tell me more," he said. "How did you hunt down our murderous mailman?"

"I'll tell you everything, but I happen to be starving. Can we order out?"

"Have I ever said no to that question?"

"Never. That's one of your most appealing qualities."

"Do you want Chinese?"

"Absolutely. I'm sort of in the mood for shrimp with lobster sauce." She waited anxiously for his response. But hell, if she was going to move in with him, now was the time to reveal her innermost secrets.

"Hmmm, shrimp with lobster sauce. I haven't had that in ages. But I always liked it."

She was the luckiest girl in the world, Nina thought, as she made her way over to the phone.

CHAPTER 29

The stalking story hit in a big way. *Newsday* **got it first,** as Margaret Connell had promised Artie. By the next day, even the *Times* was running descriptions of poor Henry Carr with his hat brim pulled down over his face.

But Ida Fischman had been right. The headlines with more staying power were Mundo's. POSTAL PIMP and MAIL HOOKER SCAM ran for days. The public became fascinated with the fact that an ordinary civil servant could, with ingenuity and vision, amass a fortune while his pension vested.

For it turned out that Mundo had built quite a little empire in Jonathan's building. He and the girls had been grossing six figures monthly. And with virtually no overhead. For weeks New Yorkers suggested to their spouses that they "go get a second job like Mundo the mailman."

Mundo was immediately arrested for Ray's murder. Mundo must have been wearing gloves, since the police couldn't find any prints in Jonathan's car. But they managed to come up with a few hairs and a few threads, enough to deliver a quick indictment.

Henry Carr resigned right away, although no harassment charges were brought against him. Betty filed for divorce, put her kids in boarding school and checked in to Canyon Ranch in the Berkshires for a couple of months. It was nice, she said, to have a spa up north, where you could spend the summer without turning into a lizard. Meanwhile, Henry went off to Nantucket to stay with a maiden aunt for a while.

An interim Public Advocate was appointed who kept Margaret Connell but fired Eddie Kornbluth. Eddie eventually got a job as a press agent for a rich person's wife, a woman who'd had bad luck with her last employee. At least Eddie, she reasoned, wouldn't steal her shoes. Charlotte Klein got pregnant, married an Israeli and went off to Tel Aviv to have her baby. Kristen gave up The Life and became a hair colorist. She found that she could get her clients in and out more quickly than she used to. And she could charge them almost the same.

The one who really took it in the neck was Jonathan's landlord. With the termination of Mundo's operation, the building's vacancy rate went way up. Most of Mundo's girls moved out, since they couldn't carry the apartments on their own. And the rental market, though stronger than it had been in years, wasn't good enough. It was impossible to re-let those apartments at the kind of rents that the hookers had been paying. Besides, the stigma of a dead doorman and the tabloids' description of the building as a glitzy high-rise kept many potential tenants away.

Circumstances that were unfortunate for the landlord proved to be fortunate for Jonathan. Because by the time his lease came up for renewal, the landlord was so desperate to keep him that he offered to chop a full hundred dollars off the monthly rent. This pleased Jonathan but annoyed Nina, who found that the new lower rent undercut her argument that they should relocate.

Nina had moved in, displaying amazingly little neurotic

behavior. She had waited a few weeks, then resumed her campaign to find a new apartment.

"Where do you want to move to?" he asked her one evening, when she had started in again.

"Where do you think? Across the park."

"Oh, please. Upper West Side, Upper East Side, they've become nothing more than alternate sides of the park. There's no difference anymore. You have a Banana Republic here, a Gap there, an Ottomanelli's Café down the block. It's all the same. Face it, Nina, Isaac Bashevis Singer is dead. You're clinging to a past that no longer exists."

She didn't want to hear it. "Well, where would you move if you had your choice?"

"Someplace with more lenient alternate side of the street parking requirements. I hear that there are parts of the city where you only have to move your car once a week."

"Where?" Nina sneered. "Staten Island?"

"What's wrong with Staten Island? There are some great old Victorians out there."

"Keep in touch," Nina said.

"C'mon. My parking situation is killing me." He sighed. "I really miss Ray. And you're no help at all. You're a complete failure as an alternator."

"A what?"

"An alternator. That's what they call the guys who move your car from side to side. Didn't you know that?"

"No."

"And you claim to be a native?"

Nina had adjusted well to living with Jonathan's cat, feeding and cleaning Kitty Litter without complaint. But she had refused to take any responsibility for the car. She idly considered starting an argument, the way she might consider starting a loaf of sourdough bread. But she had no starter left in her at the moment.

"But," Jonathan said cautiously, "I do think we should move at some point."

"You do? Why?"

"Well, don't you think we might need more space? Eventually, that is."

"Maybe." He was dancing around, but she knew what he meant. Neither of them could come out and say it. Babies. The B word was harder to say than the M word.

She had to admit it was pretty pathetic. Here she was, living with this man, for Godssakes, and neither of them could bear to address the issue of whether or not to have children. In the grand scheme of things, from an eternal point of view, she supposed that procreation was the single most important act a human being could commit. Or fail to commit. Whether to order an appetizer or how short to hem your skirt were mere dust motes in comparison. And yet here were Nina and Jonathan, nervously making vague references to unspoken possibilities.

Hell, she plunged in. "Do you want to have a child? Is that what you mean?"

"Uh, well, uh, well . . ." He stuttered for a while. Then he finally pushed himself into the water alongside her. "Well, yeah. I mean, isn't that what all this is about?"

So that's what this is all about, Nina thought. Sometimes I wonder. But she just said "Yeah, I guess."

They both exhaled. The conversation had ended. They had each only put a toe in, really. It hadn't exactly been an endurance test, hammering out the hard issues, swimming the English Channel. But there they sat, proud of themselves. Because they knew that in their own tiny, tentative, toe-immersing way, they were moving the plot along.